The Passion of
Estelle Jordan

The Passion of
Estelle Jordan

Ernest Hebert

Viking

VIKING
Viking Penguin Inc., 40 West 23rd Street,
New York, New York 10010, U.S.A.
Penguin Books Ltd, Harmondsworth,
Middlesex, England
Penguin Books Australia Ltd, Ringwood,
Victoria, Australia
Penguin Books Canada Limited, 2801 John Street,
Markham, Ontario, Canada L3R 1B4
Penguin Books (N.Z.) Ltd, 182–190 Wairau Road,
Auckland 10, New Zealand

First published in 1987 by Viking Penguin Inc.
Published simultaneously in Canada

LIBRARY OF CONGRESS CATALOGING IN PUBLICATION DATA
Hebert, Ernest.
The passion of Estelle Jordan.
I. Title.
PS3558.E277P37   1987   813'.54   85-41090
ISBN 0-670-80947-0

Printed in the United States of America by
Fairfield Graphics, Fairfield, Pennsylvania
Set in Primer

This book is dedicated to battered people everywhere:
may they find their peace.

Author's Note

This is the fourth in what I expect to be a five-novel series revolving around the fictional town of Darby, New Hampshire. Estelle—the Jordan "Witch"—was introduced in *A Little More Than Kin* and appeared in *Whisper My Name*, and her story in this book will conclude my explorations of the clan, a people both a part of and apart from society.

Contents

The Passion of
Estelle Jordan

1

A Voice

The Witch stepped out onto the second-story landing from her apartment in the auction barn, and lit her corncob pipe. Usually, she didn't smoke until the sun was falling over the hills, but at changes of seasons she might draw down half a bowl before lunch, not enough to get her stoned, just enough to put a halo of yellow around things. Another Jordan might have turned to the bottle, but not the Witch. She hated booze. It was sewage, running through the Jordan bloodlines like shit in a stream. With a wave of her hand she made as if to shoo the spring breeze as it caressed her skin. She didn't trust touch, even a touch from nature; every touch was a frisk, somebody wanting something. Not a house in sight—glad for that. Fields, trees, even the air—greening up. All of Darby, all of Tuckerman County—greening up. Oppressive. To distract herself from the green, she invited the toke to sharpen the sounds of the countryside: birds (yammering like cheapskates), the wind (ambling through the trees like a satisfied pickpocket), the highway (moaning as if the rub of tires hurt), and, finally, a tractor-trailer truck (swearing slowly through its gears). She watched it chug over the hill and then down onto the straight-away that ran past the auction barn. It picked up speed and vanished into new foliage. Its power sent a subtle trembling through her, and without thinking about it she ran her hands

1

across her blouse and down to her hips, as she might when posing for a customer. ("I like a man with a bulge in his billfold," she would say.)

Her eyes swept back along the highway. The road and the sky were milky and yellow in the late-morning light. Everything else was green or becoming green. She sucked on her pipe. Her eye stopped roaming an instant before her mind registered a thought: something wrong, nature's makeup smudged. A gleam in the trees, a black-and-silvery gleam. What did it matter to her? She turned away and walked down the wooden staircase. It shuddered under her footfalls. Like everything else built by Jordan men, it was rickety, whacked together, barely functional.

Piled against the barn were discarded electric stoves and refrigerators. It had been a couple of years since her son Ike had died—shot to death by an unknown assailant—but his son Critter had yet to move everything out, even though he had closed down Ike's auction business. The Witch guessed the white goods would be there long after she was gone.

The four-wheel-drive Subaru she'd absconded with when old man Williamson died was the only car in the parking lot. The mud was drying out. Soon it would be dusty. She wished Critter would pave it. She decided to have a look at the garden before leaving. It hid behind some briars. Delphina Jordan, Critter's wife, had broken the soil here, raising tomatoes, peas, green beans, and summer squash. The Witch grew only one crop, marijuana. Old man Williamson, who had been opposed to her vice, nonetheless had advised her how to plant it. "You put the toke in the ground when you put the tomatoes in the ground, day after Memorial Day, when the danger of a killing frost has passed."

The sight of the garden, dark and moist, awaiting her hand, changed her inside, tore away the protective shield of her anger. She was all soft now—could be hurt. She had to resist an impulse to kneel in the dirt. She remembered a young, shabby girl, violated, weighed down with children, bone-weary from hours in a shoe shop. She could see that poor girl now, shaking, lonely, sick to her stomach from ugliness (although at the time she didn't know that's what it was that sickened the human heart: ugliness). She remembered the stink of the shop. It soaked her clothes, infiltrated the pores of her skin. The stink was a mixture of smells, the burnt smell of raw leather, the acid smell that was the ache of machines, the nauseating smell that was the toil of human bodies. She had turned to the factory to get away from whoring. Oliver had said, "Go ahead. Try some real work for a change." Six months later, defeated by the shoe shop, she went back to her profession. After that any physically demanding labor filled her with loathing and sadness. But when old man Williamson had introduced her to gardening, he had made the work seem like exercise or play, even worship, an activity to make a person affectionate, strong, whole. With Williamson's spirit in mind, she'd made all sorts of plans to raise vegetables when she moved into the auction barn. But when she'd felt the raw touch of the earth, all the work fears returned, so she planted only what she needed.

The Witch knew something was wrong from the moment her car pulled out of the long driveway of the auction barn onto the state road. She felt more than saw the flash of black and silver, the way she felt betrayal in a man's eyes in the split second before he raised his hand to strike her. It was the same black-and-silver gleam she'd seen in the woods from the landing, a black Trans Am, the kind young men drove. It had been waiting for her, and as soon as she had turned toward Tuckerman, it had jumped on her tail.

She drove on, watching in the rearview mirror. The Trans Am kept a distance, just far enough away so she could not see

3

the face of the driver. She speeded up. The Trans Am speeded up. She slowed. The Trans Am slowed. She felt almost as if she controlled it, even while she understood it controlled her, since it was the Trans Am (her mind welded car to driver) that chose the measure of distance between them.

"What's your game, sonny?" She spoke as if the Trans Am could hear her; if he were close, she had no doubt she could wither him with a witch's look.

Had to be a kid. No grown man would own one of those cars; no grown man would follow an old whore. Some kid driving, following, maybe drinking, for sure thinking, thinking, jacking off to beat hell, she bet. She was mad. Not because she had anything against masturbation or against someone taking pleasure from thoughts about her. What angered her was not being compensated for that pleasure.

The Trans Am roared up until it was only a few feet from the rear bumper of the Subaru. She saw now in the rearview mirror that the driver was wearing a black mask. Before this had time to sink in, the Trans Am fell behind her a bit, accelerated, then passed her, its metal skin almost (it seemed) scraping her own skin. In a few seconds, it was gone, rocketing ahead at speeds she herself had never known.

Something happened then that she did not expect and could not have explained. Her anger passed, replaced by another feeling both familiar and alien, a tangle of premonition and memory, desire and terror. She twisted the car mirror so she could see her face. It was old. She looked at her hands on the steering wheel. They resembled bandages that needed changing. She imagined herself aging—next year, sixty, then seventy, eighty, ninety, a hundred, and beyond, each age presenting itself as a mental photograph until there was nothing but bones, cobwebs, and green dust, and suddenly she was young again, beautiful, soft, fresh. The images faded, while the feeling that

4

brought them on drove deeper into her. She bit the side of her palm, to experience with her mouth the trembling of her hand.

On the outskirts of Tuckerman, she turned into a dirt drive almost as long as the one at the auction barn. At the end was a two-story wood-frame house that had been so many years without paint the clapboards were weathered as barn siding: her son Donald's place. In the yard was a single elm tree, dead, and some grass but no lawn as such, some brush but no bushes, nothing planted by a hand. The view from the house consisted in all directions of junked cars, parked on the undulating acreage as if by nature, that is, in no particular order, left not even by the whim of the fellows who parked them but by convenience with no respect or attention to an idea of order: this the Witch recognized as Jordan order.

Kin and kinship—no escape. She had kin everywhere in Tuckerman County and nowhere else. Nothing she could do about it. She was in the kinship; it was in her; she was here; it was here. No escape. But she did not want to escape. The kinship, bad as it was, was preferable to the common run. She accepted this proposition without question, out of habit, an idea as deeply ingrained in her as the will to breathe or dream.

When she got out of her car, she scanned the area hoping to catch sight of Donald, for she knew he wouldn't be in the house at this time of day. He'd probably be in the shop, a four-bay concrete-block garage where Donald and his crew of kin worked on cars. No women were allowed in the building, but there was always the possibility she might get a glimpse of him in the junkyard or walking to his tow truck.

Donald Jordan was known locally as Tuckerman County's most creative swearing man, a character, intelligent perhaps, but ignorant and backward. But to the Witch and to others in the Jordan clan Donald was a pillar in their community, level, stable, almost kindly in his rebuffing ways, somewhat shrewd in business dealings, a man with deep knowledge of the kinship, a man to respect. He was her only living child, and she was proud of him and proud of herself for having given him life. Yet Donald was also a sore on her soul that would never heal. She'd had Ollie at sixteen, Ike at seventeen, Donald ten months later when she was still seventeen. She was just a child herself, and she couldn't handle another baby. Oliver didn't want him—Donald wasn't his; only Ollie was his. The state took Donald away from her. He was raised first in foster homes and later by this kin or that, whoever would offer succor. Of her children, he was the least ill-made. The Witch suspected he had turned out well for the very reason that he had been kept away from her during his formative years. He didn't call her mother or by her name, Estelle; like any other Jordan, he called her Witch, and his coolness toward her was a constant punishment. It was a punishment she accepted as her due and without a whimper, except that she longed to tell him, "Think what you will of this old whore, but don't hate that poor girl that bore you; mourn for her." But of course she could never say such a thing, and he could never hear it even if she could say it.

She watched a small boy dash from the house, run around the tree, and then vanish into the wilderness of junk cars, there, presumably, to play. Moments later a woman called through the screened door of the back porch. "Rickey...Rickey? Rickeeeeee?...Time to go....Right now....Or else." It was a weak summons, full of concern but with no authority, and the boy did not respond to it.

The Witch recognized the voice of Noreen Cook, a distant cousin. In the sense that everyone in the kinship knew all about everyone else in the kinship, the Witch knew all about Noreen. She was among the lowest of the low in the clan: a woman who didn't work steady, two kids, no husband. Until now the Witch had never paid Noreen any attention, but her encounter with the Trans Am had triggered a change ... in her ... the world ... something ... somebody. In Noreen's voice she heard a voice within a voice. She knew absolutely that the second voice (that she realized did not exist except in her imagination) would hold great importance for her, although it puzzled her why she should entertain such a strange thought. The odd suspicion dawned on her that Noreen possessed something that belonged to her.

They met on the porch. Noreen was frail without being bony, her skin fair without being washed out; her whiteness contrasted with the Witch's darkness; her hair was the color of dried grasses.

"I wish you'd cast a spell on that boy of mine, because mind he won't," Noreen said.

"Smack his face." The harshness in the Witch's tone made Noreen wince.

"I can't bear to lay a hand on him, and he knows it." Noreen quivered but did not move, like a dog that expects to be punished.

Noreen: wasting herself on ungrateful men, how stupid, how unconscious. It would be a pleasure to smack *her*. In the conjuring lens of her mind, the Witch watched herself raise her hand and bring it down against Noreen's prissy little mouth. So she was shocked by the sound of her own voice, soft and kind, and by the words she uttered: "Boys are hard to raise— they got no smarts."

Her expression, too, must have softened, because across Noreen's face spread the joy and courage of one forgiven by a superior.

"You have ahold of your life?" Noreen held up a tiny, doubled fist.

A flicker of anger flared in the Witch, and she slighted the question with a smirk. But Noreen took it as a smile of encouragement.

"I wish ... I wish ... I wish somebody would take hold of my life," Noreen said.

The Witch enveloped Noreen's fist with her own hands. *Squeeze her, squeeze the stupidity from her.* But she did not squeeze. She opened Noreen's fist, as if setting free a bird. With that, something passed between the Witch's anger and her kindness. Strange and incomprehensible it was, a mirror appearing out of nowhere, reflecting not a recognizable image but a slash of silver light; then, nothing.

Noreen sensed something of the strangeness in the Witch. "Gee," she said.

With no further talk the Witch and Noreen joined the other Jordan women in the kitchen—Donald's wife Tammy, her daughter-in-law Jayne, and Delphina Jordan, Critter's wife. As in all Jordan houses, children came and went, toddling on floors perpetually gritty.

The women sat around a big polyurethaned pine-board table, littered with coffee cups, dirty plates, two ashtrays almost overflowing, cereal boxes, a blow dryer, toys, a *People* magazine, last week's *TV Guide,* and other items. There was hardly room for an elbow. The Witch never noticed the clutter, but she was aware in an odd way, like a grief, of the cigarette-burn scars on the table and dents made by children.

The Witch took her place at the head of the table, where a chair had been left for her. Noreen sat off to the side in a straight-back chair against the wall.

"Rickey won't come in," Noreen announced her troubles.

"Kids—you have 'em to keep you sane, and then they drive you crazy," said Tammy, whom the Witch rated as good-natured with a brain capacity the size of a hedgehog's.

"Call one of those lazy men to fetch him." Delphina Jordan emphasized the word *lazy*, and pointed at the CB mike hanging from the wall.

Tammy and Jayne tittered in agreement. Noreen wasn't sure whether to take the suggestion seriously.

With her long, bleached-blond hair, her huge breasts, and her voluptuous body full with child, Delphina was an impressive sight. By Jordan standards, she was magnificent.

"Still waitressing?" Delphina addressed Noreen.

"I took the day off. Split shifts are killing me. On my feet all the time. I'd give anything for a job where I could get off my feet."

The Witch scorned Noreen with a laugh. If there was anyone who had made a living off her feet it was the Witch. All the women but Noreen shifted uncomfortably in their chairs. Noreen seemed about to say something, thought better of it, then stared blankly ahead, in protective, enforced semi-catatonia. The women picked up on the conversation they had been having before the Witch entered the room.

"Donald says to me, he says, 'Don't call the garage on the CB—it's for emergencies,'" Tammy reported. "I says to him, I says, 'Well, why our whole lives is an emergency.' He says to me, he says—"

"I'll call him and ask him the time of day." The Witch exercised her right to interrupt Tammy.

"I believe you would," Tammy lied.

The Witch was bluffing of course, and the other women, except perhaps for Noreen, knew she was bluffing, but none would call her on it.

The Witch's ascendancy within the clan was of a special kind. It was not based on her ability to provide succor, but on her character and on the life she'd lived. While no one talked to her about her past, she knew much of it was well-known in the kinship and much discussed behind her back. They could see in her what the kinship was, in all its terrible intimacy.

Little Ollie, the Witch's great-grandchild, ran to the Witch and demanded attention. She hoisted him up and without meaning to looked deeply into his eyes. They squirmed with the wormy markings of the Jordan clan. The child, aware now of the eyes of the Witch (his own eyes full of pain and experience in the kinship), let out a single scream, like an animal caught in a trap. The Witch put him down and Ollie ran to Delphina, his mother.

She called for a sweet, and Jayne responded by fishing out a half a doughnut from under the *TV Guide*. Delphina shoved it in Ollie's mouth, and the boy quieted, crawling under the table with his prize.

Everyone was silent for a moment, and then Delphina let out an exaggerated moan, to gather her audience. She patted her great tummy, and said, "I'll be glad when this son comes into the world, because for all the world I'm tiring of carrying him."

"How you know it's going to be a him?" the Witch asked.

"I just know."

"You just know how to make boys, do you?" The sarcasm in the Witch's tone elicited supporting laughter from Tammy and Jayne.

Delphina folded her arms and let them fall on her belly, a pose that said, "Okay, you win, Witch, but I'm still royalty."

She treats her pregnancy like it was money in the bank— and she's right to do so, thought the Witch. Delphina probably would have a dozen kids, and with the birth of each she would grow stronger. The Witch saw her as a rival.

Why do you worry about such things? the Witch asked herself. By the time Delphina has all those children and the ascendancy they'll bring her, you'll be long dead or locked up in the loony bin like Romaine. The Witch couldn't remember the last time she'd thought about her mother, and now without warning she appeared in her mind, heavy-bodied and raven-haired, washing the child Estelle's face in cold streamwater. Romaine, why couldn't you have had the courtesy to die like Daddy? *Maybe when she passes on she'll take the ache she left me with.*

Romaine Jordan was in Concord, only seventy miles from Darby. But the Witch hadn't seen her mother in thirty years. Nothing scared the collective minds of Jordans like mental illness, and when Romaine had been committed to the state mental hospital, she might as well have been banished from the kinship. No Jordan would think of visiting kin in an institution, out of fear for his own sanity and concern for his fellow Jordans: mental illness was catching and Jordans were susceptible.

The women jabbered on, the Witch giving them less and less of her attention. Finally, bored, she left them without excusing herself, walking to the back porch. The sun was warm on the unpainted wooden floor, and she could feel the heat reflect up under her skirt. The air against her face was still a little cool, and the contrast of temperatures excited her. She went outside and sat on the steps, looking out on the junk cars, seeing them, but taking no heed of them. She was there less than a minute when Noreen joined her.

The Witch fixed her with a glare, and Noreen winced slightly. Noreen spoke a word then the Witch rarely heard, her own name.

"Estelle—Estelle?" The second "Estelle" was a barely audible whisper. *Who calls me, speaking from Noreen's throat?*

Below, in the maze of derelict automobiles, was Donald's shop. The Witch pointed at it. "Down there," she said. "That's where you'll find your Rickey. When they can, boys play near men."

11

"Right now, I don't care—let him do what he wants. I'm sick of my children—they tire me; I'm sick of my feet—they hurt me; I'm sick of work, and I'm sick of never having no money." On the verge of tears, Noreen brushed away spits of blond hair that fell onto her forehead. It was the kind of gesture that warmed a man, the Witch noted.

She felt no pity for Noreen, but rather a kind of desire, not sexual exactly, but close to it. Noreen smelled faintly of her own sweat and perfume, and her skin had the newness of the spring's growth.

"So, you disturb me for advice," the Witch said.

"I need an income and some time to myself," Noreen said. "I've been thinking. Your business. Maybe you could show me, get me started."

"You want to become a whore." The Witch dragged out the word *whore*—"*ho-wahhhhh*."

Noreen sat stock-still, halted by the sudden turn of the Witch's tone, hard and cruel.

The Witch went on, dropping her voice to a malicious hush. "There ain't a job in Tuckerman County would appeal to you, Noreen. You're lazy and horny; you figure why not take money for what you've been giving away. You look at me and you say to yourself, 'Now there's a woman's made a living on her back.'"

The Witch shifted her body so that it almost touched Noreen's. "But the world has changed, Noreen. It's not what it was when I started out, my skin soft and silky as the petal of a rose. In those days, single girls were shy to give it, and married ladies often served it cold. No man wants cold cuts for his main meal. So, they would come to me, hungry for something hot. But today good, stout fellows don't need to pay no whore. They get it for free and they get it hot. The leftovers is what you're going to get—fellows with problems, fellows who want to hurt you, or who got private ideas about sex that

12

will make you want to go to church and ask, 'Why do You allow this?'"

"Allow?" Noreen mumbled the word.

"You have to understand," the Witch said, "this old whore makes her living on old boys she's known for years, fellows with troubles you're too young to understand, like sickness and dying and loss. They talk more than do; they need to talk it out, to talk it up. I know when to listen, when to speak, and when to take my teeth out."

"Old men?" Noreen said with loathing.

"Once they get past your petal-soft skin, Noreen, they're going to see you ain't worth pissing on."

Although her words were cruel, the Witch had dropped her voice to a whisper, almost kindly.

"Something 'else, Noreen. I've seen your boyfriends. You don't pick 'em too good. You think they hurt you now, just wait until they're paying for it. Your problem, Noreen, is you're dumb; you got no judgment; you got no experience. All you got is an idea to improve yourself and an itchy twat for talent. It's not enough today. Today you got to have an education or wisdom. You ain't never going to have either."

Noreen began to weep softly. "I know what you're saying," she said. "You're trying to save me."

The Witch drew away.

When she had finished crying, Noreen shouted, "Rickey! Rickey!" and miraculously the boy came running. Noreen smiled at the Witch in gratitude.

The Witch smiled inwardly. Noreen would have been tough competition. Men liked young stuff, especially young stuff as naturally dumb as Noreen. As a dog's hunger was excited by the smell of a rotting carcass, so was the lust of a man excited by "naturally dumb."

Noreen and the boy left hurriedly. The Witch watched them sputter off in a yellow Volkswagen bug.

13

The Witch lunched, gossiped, and played some with little Ollie. The child seemed to have forgotten that he had been frightened earlier by his great-grandmother's eyes. With no more than a "See-ya-later," she left at her usual time, around two. Jordans came and went with bare amenities. They rarely shook hands, rarely embraced, and never exchanged more than a word or two of greeting or farewell. Jordans appeared and disappeared from a scene. They reserved touch for important activities, such as sex and fighting; their ceremonies of succor and ascendancy passed among them invisible and unspoken, if not unfelt.

Outside, the Witch took a long look at the garage where Donald worked. The building was plain, unmarked, and unpainted, like a beaver lodge in its dismalness. On impulse, she began to walk toward the garage.

Of her children, Donald was the only one living and the only one who had risen above her in the kinship. He owned ascendancy over her not because she needed him for succor (she needed no one); not because she feared him (although she did and was happy to feel that fear); not because of the shame of having abandoned him (although the shame was there, like grinding sand on a pair of knees); but because she sought to protect him from herself. She had a feeling, not so clear that she could have explained it in words, that her love was a killing thing. There was a curious power latent in this idea, for if she should ever want ascendancy over Donald, it would be there for the taking. She had no such intention. She was content to surrender her ascendancy to him.

Three of the garage bays were open. She couldn't bring herself to go in. Donald had a rule: no women in the shop. So she stopped at the closed door, where she couldn't be seen by the men inside, and she listened. She heard metal clashing, compressors passing gas, engines revving, and screechings whose sources she could not identify. Sometimes the sounds

14

were tidier, tinklier—wrenches turning bolts into place, hammers pinging metal, air whistling as it left tires, fenders responding almost with a sexual *uh!* as they were hit by rubber mallets. She heard muffled discussions of the current job spiced with Donald's creative swearing. She heard no talk about people, events, sports, or movies. No music played because Donald banned radios from the shop.

No women, no impressions allowed from the outside—Donald's rules made perfect sense to the Witch. In his work life, which consisted of perhaps all but two hours of his every waking moment, Donald had narrowed the world to a dent.

The closed door suddenly roared open, sliding upward on its tracks, and the Witch stood revealed before the maw of the garage. She had an image of herself being run over by a car, but she did not move. Neither car nor man approached the door. It had opened for no reason that she could fathom. She could see men working now, but they were all busy and did not notice a woman standing in the bright light of the day, only one step from the inside of the shop.

She watched Donald inspect a piece of metal, turning it over and over in his hands. She understood. The knowledge of the mind was useless without the knowledge of the hands. At eye level beside him was a welding torch, a hose uncoiling from it. Because the torch hung from a wire the Witch could not see, it resembled a snake about to strike. She imagined herself reaching out, interwining with the snake, suffocating it in her bosom to prevent it from striking its fangs into the neck of her son.

Working on cars dirtied a normal man. Grease streaked his hands and face with black marks; grit got under his fingernails and over time wore into the folds of his skin. Eventually, even his sweat appeared soiled. Not Donald. He didn't look dirty; he looked reconstituted. Exposure to steel and the fallout of automotive lubricants had given his skin a permanent, metallic sheen. He changed his blue overall jumpsuit so rarely it had ceased to resemble denim but rather some rare cloth—stiff, dark, slick as black light reflected off water. Standing perfectly still, his welder's mask tipped on top of his head, he might have been a model for a statue honoring the mechanics of America.

Shadow obscured his face; she wanted to see it before she left, assure herself that this was really Donald, her only living son. But she dared not step into the shop, dared not call out his name. She waited, stupefied as Noreen had been minutes ago. As Donald reached for the torch, it appeared to the Witch that it was the torch that had snapped at the hand, and now shook it. A light cut across her eyes. Fire spewed from Donald's hand; hand and fire became one. He turned toward her then, slowly, head bowed, as one asking for succor. She strained to see his face. But he flipped the welder's mask down, and it was as if he had no face, as if the flesh of him had petrified into the things he worked—metal, glass, rubber, plastic, petroleum. The torch cut into metal. The light whitened until it was blinding; sparks flew. She felt a surge of desire for the light. She reached out to touch it even as she backed away from the garage, heading for her car. In that moment, she recognized the voice she had heard in Noreen's voice; it was her own from years ago.

2

Mired

"Well?" Avalon Hillary turned to his wife, sitting in her rocking chair. She looked strange to him, no knitting in her lap, no cookbook, no newspaper. Nothing.

Melba smiled faintly at him. That was a surprise. Usually she'd sound off at him if he tried to butt into her thoughts.

"There's something about the way you're sitting—all loose," Avalon said. He was going to add "your hands unoccupied," but that was foolish.

"I'm just tired," she said.

He found himself uncomfortable, as if the air in the room were draining away. He wanted to say to Melba, "Wouldn't you like to just get away, suffer our old age in Florida or Arizona, anyplace but New Hampshire?" Instead he said, "I'm heading on out to dig that ditch."

"Maybe you could sit with me for a minute or two," she said.

"Melba, I've been trying to find the time to do this job for weeks now." It surprised him that he was sharp with her.

"Of course you have," she said.

These last words sat in Avalon's mind as he hurried outside into the bright spring sun. It wasn't what she had said that unsettled him somewhat, but the way she had said it, completely without sarcasm. Is that my gal? he asked himself. Something told him to rush back into the house, but he continued to walk on. He was a farmer, and work came before any urges a man might have. By the time he reached the backhoe, parked on the concrete slab at the lower edge of the barn, he had dispatched Melba from his thoughts and turned his attention to the job at hand.

Avalon, astride his backhoe—"like a goddamn Wild West cowpoke," he said to himself—began digging a drainage ditch in the field that unrolled from his house and barn like a wrinkled green carpet. He didn't really need to dig the ditch. The low spot had been there for generations of Hillary holsteins. When it rained they avoided it. No problem. But it had rankled him for years: unproductive land. And, too, he wanted an excuse to mount the backhoe—Yankee cowpoke, *eeyaha!* He shouted the exclamation in his mind. From the sitting height of the backhoe his fields seemed thicker, lusher, greener. And his girls (Avalon's nickname for his cows) seemed to pay him more attention when he had the backhoe to bulk out his pathetic human form. Ma-ooed in appreciation of his efforts to make them content, they did. Oh, sure. His daughter Julia now hogged into his thoughts. "They are not your girls, Daddy. They are cows—animals. Even if they were human, they still would not be your girls, because they are adults. They would be women. A cow is not a female person; a woman is not a girl." People these days twisted around the things you said into the goddamnedest knots.

Avalon did not dwell upon this thought, nor did he dwell upon his sense of exhilaration at driving the backhoe, the sudden apprehension of natural things upon his nostrils (the smell of the river through the fumes of the backhoe). Thoughts, emotions, memories zipped through his mind with the ease of his old Buick speeding on I-91 on the other side of the river. Not that Avalon Hillary was an insensitive or unreflective man. Quite the opposite. His wife Melba would say, "You do brood," and he would answer, "I do brood." It was just that Avalon

Hillary was of little importance to Avalon Hillary. What was important, what Avalon brooded about, was the farm.

It was acknowledged locally that the Hillary farm had for generations produced the best holstein herds in Tuckerman County. Yet Avalon took no pride in his standing among his peers. Rather, it was a burden to him. "Keeping up" was how Avalon put it to himself, keeping up with the legacy of his father and grandfather, keeping up with the demanding spirit of the farm itself. He, Avalon Hillary, was hardly a being unto himself. He was but one part of the farm, no more important than a cow or a shed or a tractor or a clod of earth. A cow made milk, a shed provided shelter, a tractor did work, a clod of earth grew feed, and a man schemed out the factors, the "work and worry." He did this not for himself, but for the farm. It seemed to Avalon that after sixty years he'd had not a rich life or a poor life, but no life at all, except insofar as his life was a cell in the greater life of the farm. A beast the farm was, wiggly with life and death, and yet unfeeling, unthinking; a blob, an idea; critical and judgmental by the fact alone of its being.

Thank God for Melba. She had warmed him, steadied him, and, most important, listened to him. He was a man other men looked up to, came to for help, or held at arm's length as a rival. He wasn't naturally chummy. He'd had plenty of work and worry, but no one of his own sex to sound off to. So he talked to Melba. Sometimes she said, "No, you shouldn't do that" (usually he ignored her advice); sometimes she heartily agreed with him (not often) and he swelled inside; sometimes she laughed in his face; sometimes she patted him as if he were a beloved dog; sometimes she never said a word. She had become his friend, his only friend. She had her own prob-lems—the bad ticker, the children who seemed content to keep miles between themselves and the farm (they sensed it wanted to consume them), the sheer loneliness of a large, empty house, secret hurts from a rough-and-tumble upbringing. He knew these things in her, and yet he could offer little more than his presence for comfort. He could tell her his problems, which of course were the problems of the farm, but he could not listen to her problems. She understood a man could not receive a burden while he unburdened himself, so she bore up and kept a silence about her own troubles. He knew her and he knew nothing about her. Face it—he'd failed her. He wished somehow to make it up to her, to understand her as she understood him, if not for justice's sake, for no better reason than to satisfy his curiosity about her. Melba, you know this poor soul—now tell me about thee. There was only one way to accomplish this—get out from under the farm. Then maybe he could pay her some attention.

But their chance had gone by. Some big business group had approached him. Wanted to put up a shopping mall in his fields. Asked him what he'd take for his acreage. He'd quoted a staggering sum. They said okay. The thought of the money had ridden over the ghosts of his father and grandfather and over the voice of the living, demanding farm. Nor, surprisingly, had he felt any guilt about selling out. Merely relief. He'd done his duty all those years, so he didn't owe the farm anything, and there had been so much money involved the practical thing to do was take it. If nothing else, Hillary men were practical-minded. His father and grandfather would have done the same thing, taken the money, although he suspected they would have criticized him for doing so. Town politics had done him in, that and bad luck. After a town vote had defeated a proposal to rezone the land, the Magnus people had left and built their mall in Tuckerman.

He was right back where he started, except dairy farming, which had been difficult to begin with, now was agony for him. He had put the place up for sale, but the legal heap surrounding the mall issue had composted and composted, and the heat from it had scared off potential buyers. He had no choice but to continue draining udders for a market glutted with dairy products. Work and worry had become a crucifix across his shoulders. Yet he worked on, worried on—did his best for the farm. He knew no other way. There was something in him that could not stand to do badly. As long as it was his farm, he'd push, push, push, make it a grand farm. What sickened him most was that he had shifted some of the weight of the crucifix to Melba. Dear wife, I'm sorry, and I heartily promise to amend my life.

He had reached the low spot, the backhoe bucking and belching all the way. He stood up, straddling the metal seat, and perused the sitation. Not that he didn't know what he was going to do. He had mulled over this job many times, along with maybe six or seven thousand other jobs that should get done but didn't need to and that therefore probably wouldn't. The last thing he'd think about before drifting off to sleep at night would be how to do a particular job, particularly one that didn't have to get done, the had-to-be-dones being no bringers of sleep. But now that he was about to do the actual work, he'd give the land a long look. He was a cautious man, even while he was a daring one. (He brooded his way toward decision, never did anything rash, but he did like to experiment. Once, he'd volunteered his cows when a university fellow had come up with a plan to remove an embryo from a superior cow and place it in the uterus of an inferior cow. The practice was routine today, and because Avalon had got in on it early he had a leg up on other farmers locally. The supercow he'd produced was worth more than the rest of the herd put together.)

The low spot, in fact, was a high spot, but a hump of earth blocked water from running off. He'd carve a three-foot-deep trench through the hump for forty feet or so. He should start on the dry side, work his way through the hump, finally chew out the last dam of earth holding back ankle-deep water. He looked hard. My, how that low spot looked inviting. Saw grasses unfit for a civilized cow; useless reeds; the puddling up of water like the pursed lips of some Upper Darby grand lady; insects hanging around like lazy teenagers—the more he thought about the low spot, the more he took it personally; unproductive land! And the more he wanted to bring it into the functioning farm.

"Goddamn," he said, settling into his saddle, gunned the engine, and started forth, heading not for the high, dry side but for the low, wet side. He felt giddy as his ancestors must have felt burning off the forest to pasture the first cows in this valley.

There was a *splook!* as the backhoe chugged into the low spot. He knew in an instant something was wrong. He'd driven this old backhoe for fifteen years, and in all the places he had brought it, it had never made a noise like that. He peered over the side and looked at the earth. The cool water was clouding up. The tires had sunk a foot and a half into muck. He tried to shrug off the feeling of impending disaster. He raised the great arm of the backhoe and scooped out some earth. It was dark, peaty. Maybe he'd save some for Melba's garden. Looked like good stuff for flowerbeds.

The trouble came when he tried to drive forward. The huge rear wheels spun, kicking up enough mud to discourage General Patton. He let up on the gas, noticing the wheels had sunk in another foot.

He was suddenly furious, blindly so—like he'd never been in his life, it seemed to him. He jumped out of the saddle, landing feet first in the muck. It grabbed his work shoes. Icy water seeped in over the tops into his socks. "Goddamn, son-of-a-goddamn, g-d." His voice petered out. He was so angry he could not even cuss properly, so angry he did another stupid thing. He put his shoulder to one of the wheels. He knew even as he heaved no man could succeed at this. Still, he heaved and heaved, and goddamn the illogic of the act; he heaved some more.

The anger left him all at once with the realization he was exhausted, dizzy. A crunching sensation radiated across his chest. He fell back into the mud, landing on his bottom like some fool. Oh, Lord, he thought, I'm having a heart attack. Can't die here, sitting down like this. He got a glimpse of the saddle of the backhoe, and an image came to his mind of a cowboy breathing his last on the desert floor. Never saw the desert, never saw anything but this g-d farm. Don't count those two weeks in the Virgin Islands, Lord—that was vacation. Oh, Lord, if you get me out of this, I'll get out from under the farm. I promise. I'll take Melba to Spain or Fitchburg, Mass., wherever she wants to go. Oh, Lord, save this poor wreck for another day. What had always been in doubt, the existence of this presumed "Lord," now seemed cemented in reality. In the wisdom of dying was God. Oh, Lord, if you want me to die like this, in the g-d mud, okay. But frankly I don't feel ready to go. Semi-prepared for death, Avalon awaited his end.

He looked up at the seat of the backhoe. Did he want to die in the saddle, did he? He imagined himself struggling up to it, singing out his last words to humanity—*Eeyahh!* No, he'd never make it up there. He'd only keel over and fall back into the mud. Crawl—I'll crawl. He might make it out of this swamp, to the house, to die in Melba's arms.

A moment later, or maybe it was five minutes, Avalon felt a little better. His vision was no longer edged in yellow. His chest hurt less; he was breathing hard, but not as hard as before. He stood, wavered a bit, and took a step forward.

By the time he reached the house, he felt tired, really weary, and sore, but he was breathing normally, and his chest no longer hurt. He was now aware how muddied up he was. Would Melba laugh at him, take pity, scold him? He was almost amused, wondering what she would think of her husband in this disreputable state, when he found her, in her rocking chair, her skin blue, no pulse—gone to her heaven.

3

The Tremor
and the Trans Am

Toothless, Estelle Jordan slowly sipped orange juice, slowly chewed mushy oatmeal, slowly drank black coffee, her eyes attending to the portable television set on the kitchen table, but her mind far away from the *Today* show or *Good Morning America*, whatever was on. It didn't matter; the TV's only reason for being was to provide company. She divided her thoughts between practical matters (cleaning up after last night's customer) and memory (a young girl feeding on soft foods and the crust of her own humiliation).

Her natural teeth had begun to rot in her teen years. A few men had complained to Oliver about the ugliness in her mouth. She too had complained—about the dull ache of tooth decay. One evening Oliver had made her drink whiskey until she was blind drunk, and then he had pulled out all her teeth. Even through the haze of alcohol, the pain had been bright and clear. But there had been something else, the skim of an emotion riding on the pain, some mixture of fear and desire, a response to the dim realization that Oliver enjoyed inflicting the pain. Pain, pleasure, mouth, Oliver: it was inevitable she should take to oral sex, that it would become her specialty, her fame.

These days she owned a fine set of false teeth that looked perfect, if unreal. The Witch never thought of them as *her*

25

teeth. They belonged to a second self, proud and stiff, who sold weed pots and dried grasses at the weekend flea market in the auction barn and who was called Estelle by her fellow vendors. The Witch wore the teeth like black lace, as a lie, a private joke—scorn on those who scorned her in their lust—and last night, as always, she had removed them to go to work.

Teeth told who you were. Jordan children grew up on sugar; Jordan children grew up without dental care. To a Jordan, a disfigured mouth was as normal and inevitable as a rusting rocker panel on a car victimized by salted roads. Never mind that the common run of Tuckerman County had healthy, cared-for teeth, and therefore a Jordan could be identified by his rotten teeth. Part of the measure of a Jordan in his own eyes was his difference from the common run, measure not by difference in quality or quantity but by difference alone.

After finishing her coffee, she washed the breakfast dishes along with a wineglass from last night's customer. He was one of her Mr. Boyntons. The meek ones paid well and they didn't hurt you and they didn't make outstanding demands, yet there was a time when she had despised them. The ones that roughed her up or gypped her earned from her a grand mash of awe and hate that, on occasion, sexually satisfied her. So, too, it went with most men, she thought. A woman gave her all, and she was a slut in the eyes of the man whom she had received; a woman withheld and whined, and, more likely than not, she'd get a marriage proposal. These days the Witch was grateful to the Mr. Boyntons and she kept her distance from the Olivers.

She tidied the kitchen, brought out the garbage, and dusted, using a pair of men's boxer shorts, size 42, her hand in the fly. She broomed the linoleum floor. She inspected the debris—lint, a gum wrapper, dirt (dirt? What was it anyway?), and the night's spores that fell in a constant rain from the dozens of hanging bunches of dried plants with which she decorated her apartment. Once, in the clutch of the toke, she had discovered the sound of the rain of spores. It was like the soft breathing of a child thinking.

There was zest in her approach to housekeeping, but the job never quite got done, the place never quite seemed picked up or clean. She abandoned tasks just short of completion.

A Jordan might have a personal idea of cleanliness and not violate the Jordan codes. A Jordan woman might or might not wash her hair, or a Jordan man might or might not wax his car. But the idea that a house should be clean and picked up made no more sense to a Jordan than it would have to a dog. It wasn't just that Jordans had no feel for cleanliness and orderliness; Jordans favored messiness. The land they occupied had so predisposed them. Jordans kept their houses, their yards, even their lives in very much the same way nature kept the woodlands of Tuckerman County. Dozens of varieties of trees grew wild, at random, competing for space and light, their growth dependent on weather, luck, and the benediction of the soil. It was a forest where the wind-twisted, the insect-ravaged, the sun-denied reached skyward with the straight, the healthy, the lovely.

After she finished with the kitchen, the Witch paused to admire her work. As usual, she felt something pressing in upon her enjoyment: an urge to disturb, to dirty up.

She put Lestoil and Comet in a bucket with some sponges and moved to the bathroom. She sponge-mopped the floor around the toilet. She could understand why men preferred to stand to piss, laziness and male vanity, but why was it that over a lifetime they never perfected their aim? In the sink was a trail of mouth-spoiled toothpaste she'd spit out, brushing her false teeth and rinsing her mouth having been the last business of the previous evening. She scrubbed the sink and rebrushed the teeth as part of the same action, as if sink and teeth were both bathroom fixtures. Her chores finished, she dabbed her face with a washcloth, and ran a comb through her hair. The

27

ERNEST HEBERT

moment she touched her face, moved toward adornment, she
could feel the whore in herself.

Late in the morning, the Witch's grandson, Critter Jordan,
paid her a visit. Critter was regular-featured, even handsome
as Jordans went. He was ambitious and pushy, but not mean.
The Witch liked him, and yet she reckoned it necessary to
establish her ascendancy over him immediately, because he
was not only her grandson but her landlord.

"You can come in, but the dog stays outside," she said while
Critter was still on the landing and before he had a chance to
speak.

"Stay—stay!" Critter commanded.

Crowbar, certain by his master's voice he was guilty of something but not of what, collapsed in a heap to await forgiveness.

The Witch didn't exactly invite Critter to sit at her dining
table, but, rather, she stopped in front of it and he took a seat.

He'd probably ask for coffee, and she didn't want to bend to
his demands, so she headed him off. "How many sugars you
take in your coffee?" she asked.

He filled the air with fiddle-faddle talk until she poured the
coffee, and then he began to back into his purpose for calling
on her.

"Fine building, this old barn," he said.

"Uh-huh." The Witch wondered what was coming.

"Fact is, there's no profit in it," Critter said. He was all
business after that, and the shift in his tone—cold, to the
point—took the starch right out of her. The truth of her position in life came down on her. Her Witch's ascendancy was
a flimsy thing, a veil. A man with property or money or a
weapon could walk through it.

He didn't come out and say so, but the Witch gathered
Critter wasn't satisfied with the weekend flea market. It didn't
pay enough in rents. He left it for her to conclude he was doing

28

the flea-market vendors a favor. He reminded the Witch he charged her no rent at all for her own flea-market space, where she sold dried plants in pots.

"I'm going to have to open a new business in the barn," Critter said.

"Uh-huh."

"Not sure what kind of business yet, but I come to see you, Witch, to offer you work, clerking, bookkeeping—whatever."

The Witch considered. She had some money saved up. If she worked part-time for Critter and he paid her medical insurance, she could retire. The old whore with no men calling— what an odd idea. If she threw in with Critter, she'd live by his succor; her ascendancy would pass to him.

"Work for kin—I think not," the Witch said. "Besides, I operate my own business."

"So you do," Critter said. He was on his feet now, on his way out. She could tell he'd never expected her to accept his offer. He'd been doing his Jordan duty toward her, warning her change was coming. At the same time, if she'd happened to go along with his plan, why he would have established ascendancy over her. As he most certainly expected, she'd turned him down, and now he could do whatever he pleased.

She watched him through the window, descending the stairs from the landing, the dog, happy now, bounding ahead of him. She watched them get into the van, roll out the driveway. As they disappeared up Route 21, she caught just a glimmer of black and silver between new leaves.

The Trans Am had followed her into Tuckerman three times since the first a week ago. She tingled at a thought of him: mask. She tried to understand the feeling he excited in her— rage and fear, but something else too. She'd had sex so early, so hard, she'd never known what it was like to be in love. Perhaps what she felt now was that feeling twisted by time. She searched about in her mind for a name for the feeling—

and found nothing but the feeling itself, uncomfortable, but irrefutably inviting.

She drove slowly out of the driveway, glancing in the Subaru's rearview mirror as it turned onto the highway. No gleam—and now he wasn't in sight. This disturbed her more than if he had jumped on her tail. All the way to Tuckerman she looked for him—and never saw him. The strange feeling subsided, replaced by the drizzle of common loss. When she arrived at Donald's place, everything seemed as it had been. She was the Jordan Witch, among her own.

"No Noreen today?" she inquired sardonically of Tammy, so as not to betray a tinge of disappointment. For some reason she wanted to see Noreen, smell her, be in proximity to her.

"Quit her job—on the loose," Tammy said.

What did Tammy mean by "on the loose"? The Witch probed. Tammy had meant nothing—neither Tammy nor any of the other women knew Noreen's plans. That made the Witch all the more suspicious. Had Noreen set up her own shop? Was Noreen recruiting her customers? Images flashed in the Witch's mind. She was slapping Noreen; she was embracing her. She was Noreen, being slapped, being embraced. Clutter of mind washed over the Witch like wreckage in a hurricane-driven sea. And then someone offered her toast, and that broke the spell. She was all right after that. As the afternoon wore on, she melded into the women at Tammy's house. When she left, the Witch was in an agreeable void, detached from memory, anticipating the drive back to Darby.

Country drives, she had come to realize, brought temporary cease-fires to the wars of the world and the wars of the self, but had little effect on her overall frame of mind. It was as if the pleasure in the drone of driving, in the contemplation of the countryside, simply sifted through her and was lost, so that when she arrived at her destination she was, so to speak, back where she started from and the wars resumed.

On the road, she marveled at the forest, leaning into the highway, or bordering a field, or seeming to be marching onto a row of houses, miles and miles of trees, wavering in the breezes or stiff and dignified in still air as old friends of the deceased paying their respects to the bereaved. Moody— the forest was moody. Oh, darling, I know how it is with you. All those creatures to born, to provide for, to shovel under.

She always noted the sky when she drove. It varied from day to day, season to season, but it wasn't the variations or even the beauty that made her take notice. It was the invitation to escape the earth. She lit her pipe and drew down the bowl like a thirsty deer at a pool. The road was a river. Her interest was not in the debris carried downstream, but in the tranquilizing rhythm of the flow.

I watch and listen, I lie in the mother's arms of my drug, I dive into myself and surface in memory: who is this? how lovely she is, I touch her, she falls, injured, she rises confused, all my fault my parents' hate, my mother, our mother, my father, our father, he drinking, hitting her from the drink, she getting back at him by sleeping around, you, I, thinking I did this, I made this bad thing happen between them, my fault, you hid in yourself as if love were a casket, you thought hard hard hard hard, figuring if I think hard about the way it should be, it will be, so let them hit me, hurt me, and my pain will make it right between them, so you invite them: hit me, and they oblige, and you understand nothing but that solution: to save heart you can't just suffer, you must suffer and die.

And the Trans Am was suddenly in her rearview mirror, and everything came together as that feeling, the twist of love, the feeling for which she had no name.

"Bastard—who bore you, the sky?" the Witch shouted into the rearview mirror.

Everything was pounding now, her heart, her womanhood,

31

the car, the colors—everything. She hadn't seen him come up on her. Had he been there all along?

"Who bore you?" she shouted again, the sound of her voice settling her somewhat.

She slowed the Subaru. The Trans Am slowed. She continued to slow until her car was only going fifteen miles an hour. The Trans Am kept the distance. A truck passed them, the *oooo-ahhhha* of its horn like the caw of some awful crow. She speeded up. The Trans Am speeded up. Soon the Subaru was going as fast it would.

She could see the auction barn up ahead, an approaching blur, the weathered siding seeming to anchor it to the ground, while the new, tan shingling on the hip roof pulled it into the building into the sky. She drove past it for a mile, then turned off the highway onto Center Darby Road, and turned off again, dropping onto River Road. She drove not by thought but by that feeling inside. The Trans Am kept the distance.

The land was different here, less rugged, less forested, rolling grassy with the river—farmland. She slowed again, the Trans Am slowed. Finally, she pulled to the side of the road beside a cow pasture of the Hillary farm. Stuck in some mud up slope in the field was a backhoe. The Trans Am sidled in behind her. She began to back up. The Trans Am backed, keeping the distance. She backed for a couple hundred yards until they were out of view of the backhoe and the pasture, and in the trees again. The Witch stepped out of her car but remained standing by the door with the engine running. The Trans Am idled, its mufflers growling. The feeling fell into the same key and rhythm as the Trans Am, as if feeling and engine were two instruments playing the same song despite the wishes of the musicians handling them. She had hoped to get a look at the mask, but the sun through the trees was on the windshield of the Trans Am and all she saw was a wavy bar of silver light. I'll stay here until death, she thought. I'll bluff him with time itself.

Minutes passed. She sensed she was winning the battle of nerves. Of course. She was the Witch—the Witch had an eye for this kind of work—look at the eye.

She thought she detected a stirring in the car. A moment later she was looking at a young man's body. He was wearing tight blue jeans, black boots, a black T-shirt, and the mask. She could see it clearly now, illuminated by a bar of light through the trees, black and shiny, clinging tightly to the features of the face, wrapping around the head like some terrible skin, two peepholes for seeing, a zipper where the mouth should be. He stood before her, a knife in his left hand, his readied prick in his right hand, knife hand still, other hand busy. The feeling fell into the rhythm of the hand. The name for the feeling formed in her mind now—the tremor; she had thus cornered the tremor; now it cornered her, increasing in intensity and power. The Trans Am ejaculated in less than a minute.

"You owe me fifty bucks!" the Witch shouted.

What happened next surprised the Witch, shocked her. The man screamed, a scream of hurt and rage ripping through mask. The tremor: he feels it too, she thought. And then she lost a moment in time. The Trans Am was gone, and she was alone, hearing birds sing, looking at the sunlight through the trees falling on the dull mat of the earth.

4

A Birth

Critter Jordan was tempted not to respond to his belt beeper when it began to sound. He was in the auction barn, drinking a beer, just sort of "inventorying," as his father would put it when he wanted to be alone. Critter liked the barn. Sometimes it seemed to him he could smell animals from long ago, cows and pigs and chickens, and he imagined he was a farmer and the animals were his: Critter's critters, feeding, mating, borning, dying—everything that people did, except simpler, quicker, with less fuss and no complaints. But he was no farmer, he knew that. He might like the idea of farming, but the idea of getting up early in the morning, why it made him sick even to contemplate.

The trouble with the barn was it didn't pay for man or beast. After his father was killed, Critter had liquidated the auction business, using the revenues to fix the roof and shore up the place so he could turn it into a weekend flea market. Even so, it failed to turn a profit. The rents he collected from the Witch and from the flea-market vendors barely covered the property taxes and expenses. He needed to make the space in the barn pay during weekdays.

The beeper continued to sound until he could no longer

ignore it. He strode outside to the van, where Crowbar, his all-breeds hound, waited. From the van, he called Delphina on the CB. "Van Man to home, Van Man to home."

"I don't feel so good." Delphina's voice crackled through the speaker.

Crowbar lay on the passenger-side seat, paws over ears. Certain noises on the CB drilled into his skull.

"Is this is it—calving time? Over," Critter said.

"Maybe it is, and maybe it ain't."

"Does it feel like the last one? Over."

"How should I know?" Annoyance with him issued from her voice. "All's I remember is I worked in the garden and it was the first day in months my lumbago didn't kick up."

"You call back when you're sure. Over," Critter said.

"Come home now! Ten-four!" shouted Delphina, and that was that.

Critter hung up the mike, started the engine of the van, checked his watch, and said to Crowbar, "Women got mean tempers."

They covered the three miles from the auction barn on Highway 21 to the house in Darby Depot in two minutes and fifty-two seconds. Critter announced the time as he barged through the rear door.

"My water just broke," Delphina said.

The front of her maternity blue jeans was dark with fluid. Critter turned his eyes away. "Why do babies always have to come at night?" he asked the dog.

Delphina called her doctor, and while still on the phone said to Critter, "Go upstairs and get the baby and my stuff. We have to go to the hospital."

She hung up and, without so much as a look back at Critter, she went to the bathroom. He stood for a moment, wondering why there was this distance between them. It hadn't been like this when Ollie was born. Delphina had had pains, and he had

35

rushed her to the hospital and she had held his hand for dear life (young Ollie's dear life, their own dear lives that he had felt the blessing of in her fingertips). He heard the shower go on, and a picture sprang to his mind of tropical downpours, jungle trees, screaming monkeys, vines. For some reason he was aware of the newness of their house, the bare, white walls—the spaciousness. He realized then why he had never been comfortable here: no mess.

"We ought to buy some pictures to put on the walls," he said, but Delphina couldn't hear above the rushing water.

Upstairs, he lifted Ollie, his two-year-old, from his crib and lay his head against his shoulder. The boy was still asleep, but he instinctively nuzzled into the crook between his father's neck and collarbone. The feeling of the boy's soft, wet, sleeping mouth against bare skin took Critter off guard. He recoiled inwardly, as one awash in the bad breath of a stranger.

Downstairs again, Critter could see the outline of his wife's bottom wet-pressed into the seat of the chair she had been sitting on when her water broke. Where did the water come from? What did it mean—"break"? Was it really water, and if so what was the water for? And if it wasn't water, why, what was it? The sight and the questions troubled him. The less a man knew about the mysteries of womanhood—the period, birth, the change of life—the better off he was. He believed, as every Jordan man believed, firmly and devoutly, that "female knowledge" tainted a man, diminished him somehow.

"Let's go," Delphina said, and they went outside to the van for the fifteen-mile trip from Darby Depot to Tuckerman County Hospital.

Once they were on the road, Critter thought that by being cheerful he might reengage himself to his wife.

"I don't get it," he said, forcing a quizzical tone. "The last time you had a baby, you were having labor pains when your water broke and you were already in the hospital."

"Every baby comes different, they say," Delphina said.

Critter frowned. Women were supposed to know about born-ing, so why the "they say"? Nor did he care for the way she addressed him, as if she wished he'd shut up and leave her alone. He felt like a taxi driver instead of her husband.

Ollie, strapped in the harness the state required, began to cry in the back seat. Delphina ignored him. Critter watched in the rearview mirror as Crowbar licked the boy's face.

"Sit!" shouted Critter, and the dog cringed, expecting to be hit.

Critter removed his handkerchief from his hip pocket and gave it to Delphina. "Wipe the kid's face where the dog kissed him," he said.

"What in the world for?" Delphina asked.

"Never mind why, just do it." Critter's tone, the unexpected authority in it, stopped her cold. She wiped the boy's face. Critter felt steadier.

He brought her to the hospital, hung around a terrible long time (terrible because he had to watch Ollie) while she checked in. He signed some papers, and then drove Ollie to Donald's house. Tammy would take good care of the boy while Delphina was in the hospital. Critter fell into a brief rapture then, relief—freedom—at having ditched the kid. He returned to the hos-pital, leaving Crowbar in the van.

The nurses had parked Delphina in the birthing room. Things had changed since Critter had been here last. The walls were papered, the bed had a wood frame, maple furniture graced the place—an end table, a lamp, a magazine rack. The idea was to make mothers-to-be feel at home by placing them in a homey atmosphere. But the effect on Critter was the opposite of what was intended. He longed for a hospital atmosphere, cold and orderly and white and stinking of ether. Not that he liked hospital rooms, but he trusted in their safety; this, a mock-up of some common-run bedroom, felt unsafe. In addition, the affected casualness gave him the impression he was supposed to stick around, help out maybe. No way, José. Delphina had tried to get him to take the wachamacallit, LaMayonnaise classes, but he had flatly refused. A man helping a woman birth a child: it was an attack not only on his manhood, but on his Jordanhood.

Delphina sat up stiffly in the bed, filing her nails. Critter might have plopped down in the chair provided, but he decided to stand, the better to escape.

"I wish you'd have some pains," he said.

"I don't want pains—why should I want pains?" She snarled at him.

For a woman about to give birth, Delphina looked mighty comfortable, acted mighty grouchy.

"It's natural to have pains," Critter said.

"Birth pains hurt—don't you understand that?" Delphina said, and Critter did not hear the fear in her voice.

He found himself uncomfortable standing still, so he leaned first on one foot, then on the other, until he was sort of pacing in place. It angered him not that Delphina was irritable but that she was irritable on the verge of having a baby. It was a bad sign. Furthermore, under these circumstances, he couldn't argue back.

Somewhere along the line she realized how downcast he was, and she said, "Critter, I'm not mad at you. I'm mad at my mother, for dying on me, for not being here."

For a second, he understood then why he had married this strong-willed woman. He, too, had lost his mother. She'd run away when he was a baby.

"Delphina," he said. "You're it: you're *the* mother."

After a while, Delphina began to wiggle and squirm and moan, and the nurses poked at her and said things Critter didn't understand—"You're fully dilated"—and, finally, the

38

doctor came in, grinning like a maniac. "Are you going to take pictures?" he asked Critter.

The doctor was crazy, and it struck him he ought to get Delphina out of there. The next thing he knew the wooden sides of the bed were removed, the furniture was shoved aside; a nurse pushed a button, and there was an *uh-uh-uh* sound as the bottom of the bed began to fall away; metal stirrups appeared. It was no bed; it was a birthing contraption. Critter backed toward the door. He'd meant to kiss Delphina good-bye, hold her hand, reassure her, and now he was slinking out like a coward. He wanted to apologize. But when he looked at her eyes, he saw apology was not only unnecessary but irrelevant. Delphina was deep into her mysteries. Critter got out.

He hung around in the hall while things happened to Delphina he wasn't aware of and didn't want to be aware of. Nurses came and went, never looking at him; he felt invisible. He went outside, walked the dog for a wee, then returned to the birthing room, but he dared not go in, dared not knock on the door. He went around the corner to the nurses' station, and asked, "Has my wife calved yet?" The nurse apparently wasn't too bright, because it took a moment for his question to sink in. "We'll let you know," she said.

Finally, tuckered out, he lay on a couch in the waiting room. He was awakened by the same nurse, who said a C-section was going to be performed on Mrs. Jordan. He thought no more of this than of a weather report on the radio, and promptly went back to sleep. Morning light opened his eyes. He arose and watched the dawn creep bloody red above the pines that bordered the hospital. He dozed on the couch off and on for another hour or so. It occurred to him he could have gone home and had a good night's sleep; it did not occur to him to check at the nurses' station on the condition of his wife.

He yawned, stretched out, and began to wander until he

found the cafeteria. He ate rather more heartily than he expected, wolfing down sausage and eggs, a doughnut, and coffee. He read a paper somebody had left on a chair and chatted with a guy waxing the floor.

"They keep these rooms clean," Critter said.

"If you work with the patients, they make you wash your hands after you go to the bathroom," the guy said.

Critter watched television in a lounge miles away (it seemed) from the birthing room. A feeling of unreality crept into him. Was he an inmate in a mental hospital? Was Delphina really here behind closed doors? Was there a Delphina?

He was on his feet now, walking fast, then running to the nurses' station.

"Has my wife calved yet?" he shouted.

"What?" The nurse frowned at him.

This was not the right nurse. Critter gathered his wits about him. "I'm Mr. Jordan, and I'd like to know what's going on with my wife."

"They've been looking for you," the nurse said.

"I had some eggs. Is she having the baby?"

"She's not having it—they're doing a C-section."

C-section—the word drew dark drapes across Critter's mind. He returned to the waiting room, picked up a news magazine, and, fascinated, read eight or nine pages before he realized nothing was sinking in. He stood, paced, gazed out the window and saw nothing.

Then the nurse called him.

The baby didn't seem to be his. It resembled an Eskimo. Ollie hadn't looked like this. Or had he? Critter couldn't remember.

They'd given Delphina something, and she was half here and half in never-never land.

"I tried it my way, but he didn't want to leave home, so they had to cut," Delphina said.

40

"Uh-huh," Critter said.

The nurse put the baby in his arms.

"You sure this one is mine?" he muttered.

"They're in such good shape after a cesarean," the nurse said. "They don't get banged up. They come out perfect."

She might as well have been speaking Arabic for all he understood.

"Boy or girl?" he asked.

"Most definitely a boy," the nurse said. "What are you going to name him?"

Critter glanced down at Delphina. He noticed her white Johnny gown, white sheets on the bed. At home they had yellow sheets and green sheets and rainbow-colored sheets, but no white sheets, and Delphina never wore white to bed.

"Del?" he called.

Delphina did not respond. She had fallen asleep.

"Dell is a nice name," the nurse said.

"No, Del is my wife's name," Critter said, still baffled by everything. "I was going to name him after me, Carlton, which is my real first name. See, we agreed if it was a boy, I'd name it. If it was a girl, she'd name it. But now I ain't so sure. I don't like the way he looks, yellow and squinty-eyed."

"That's the jaundice," the nurse said. "Nothing to worry about; most newborns do have a touch of jaundice."

"Johndiss—um. Johndiss Jordan," Critter said.

"You don't want to name a child after a disease," the nurse said.

Critter thought that over. She had a point, but he liked the way one *j* crept up on another. "All right then, Jorge. Jorge Jordan."

"A good name," the nurse said, cheer in her voice.

Like Jordans throughout Tuckerman County, Critter spoke with a thick, rural New Hampshire accent. When Critter said "Jorge" it sounded like "Jawj." Later, when he filled out the form for the birth certificate, he wrote the name the way he'd spoken it, J-a-w-j. In the clan, the boy would grow up as Jawj Jawd'n.

It wasn't until the next day when Delphina showed him her stitches that Critter understood about the C-section. Borning was a lot trickier enterprise than he'd ever imagined. He'd been right all along. It was nothing that anybody with any sense would get involved in. No wonder women developed peculiar ideas.

"I don't want more kids," he said to Delphina.

"Not for a while—I'll go along with that," she said.

"No more. Never. Understand?"

"I'll get some birth-control pills."

Somehow he hadn't expected her to say that, and he fell inside, as if he'd caught her in a lie. But he considered. He certainly wasn't about to wear safes, and the idea of more children was such a draining thing. So what else was there besides pills?

"You do that, you ask the doctor to give you some of those little pills." He couldn't bring himself to say the words *birth control*. His voice was sure, confident, yet inside he was oddly unsettled, as if he'd betrayed his wife, himself, the thing that made them one.

5

Estelle and the Witch

Although Aronson would touch her and in his own mind become intimate with her, she felt neither gratitude nor contempt for him, desire nor repugnance. She didn't even think of him as a man exactly, but as an idea—profit—made flesh. Yet at another level, the anticipation of his arrival quickened her blood. She was professional and cool, but also ready, hot, wide-awake—alive.

It was eight P.M., time to put on the whore's face. She'd wear black undergarments and purple stockings because Aronson, like most men, preferred his sex in mourning colors. It didn't make any difference to the Witch. When she was a young whore—soft, moist, pretty—she'd nonetheless had her failures with this fellow or that. She didn't listen, and that was a problem. (You listened not for his sake, since most men were too egotistical to imagine you weren't listening; you listened for your own sake, your education.) The main problem had been she sometimes wouldn't go along with the often peculiar, occasionally revolting fuss and rules a man insisted upon before the actual act itself. Eventually she learned preparations, fuss and rules, were as important as the sex. There was no right way or wrong way of sex, but only the way of the one who paid.

She buried her skirt and blouse in the hamper and, half one self, half another, stood before the bathroom sink and prepared to wash her hair. Right into her forties, people had looked at it with fear and awe. "So black," they said, and she would think, My black, no other black like it. When she brushed it, she saw gleamings of gold, brown, and red, colors of autumn.

Then a few years ago some silver hairs started coming in. She had been surprised. Somehow she'd always expected she'd pass on before the blackness of her hair. She'd pulled out the silver hairs, not because she found them unattractive but because every silver hair reminded her a black hair had been lost and made her think there was less of her. And maybe this was so. Her hair was her pride, not the Witch's pride but the pride of the deep-down dear self. The beauty of her hair, the softness of it, the flow of it was like verification that the dear self was beautiful, soft, liquid, no matter what time or man did to her body. She'd pulled silver hairs until it became impractical to do so. If she dyed her hair, the gleamings would be gone, what remained merely black—not even her black. Yet from the standpoint of her business, she had to admit gleamings meant nothing. Men saw color in great big panels to nail up; men saw black and they thought "whore," and men saw silver and they thought "old woman"; men did not see gleamings. Thus, since her hair was as much a part of her business as her person, the Witch in her favored dyeing it coal-black. But that other self, the dear self, Estelle, resisted. She saw gain as well as loss in the turning of her hair. While she might be less of the person she was, she was more the person she would be. Meanwhile, she needed gleamings. Gleamings were the energy source of magic carpets that carried women away from discouragement, depression, dislocation. But to the Witch, the turning of her hair signaled danger. The hair was not just turning, it was turning on her, like some old kinsman turning on you after years of building a grudge.

Estelle Jordan did not dye her hair; she bought a wig, keeping it in her closet in a box. Periodically she'd compare the wig with her own hair. Each time the wig seemed shinier, fuller. One day it would surpass her natural hair in beauty, and she would know it was time to pass on.

She ran water in the bathroom sink until it was short of too hot to stand, and then she let the water pour over her neck. She squeezed the shampoo gel into her hand and bent it into the wet hair. Since she washed it every day, her hair was never so much dirty as dusty. Therefore, she washed it without the violence needed to cleanse what was truly soiled. Great billowing clouds of suds pleased her hands and neck as well as her scalp. She rinsed, twirling hair in her fingers until the slipperiness went out of it.

She toweled gently, and retired to the chair in the living room from where she could watch the great sugar maple tree outside the window while she brushed her hair. The wind was coming up; the leaves on the tree seemed to tingle in the waning light. She could almost feel fluids coursing through the veins of each leaf. Deep in herself she brushed.

When her hair was dry and shiny and combed and she had enjoyed its gleamings, she stood before a full-length mirror in the living room. (She had installed the mirror to please her customers. Never mind that most of the business was conducted in the dark or in dim light, men expected mirrors in whoredom. One fellow had requested a mirror on the ceiling. "No thank you," she had said. "I don't care to look down on myself.") She peered into the mirror now and she couldn't quite believe her eyes. She had an image of herself as much younger, almost a girl—frightened, passionate, lost, and lovely, a bouquet of a person. What she saw was a woman with long, straight black hair streaked with silver, features too pronounced and strong to be considered dainty or even feminine, yet which were distinctly female and compelling. The skin was dark, glowing like a pine board that has been out in the sun. She had no makeup on, and wrinkles knifed cruelly into her eyes. The eyes themselves were boiling lava pools in which snakes writhed. She feared if she looked too deeply into those eyes she might fall into them and be consumed. Her body had filled out some, but it was still a good body. Barefoot, in white, she did not look like a whore, but like a patient in a doctor's waiting room. How plain, how homely you are, Estelle, in your white cotton underpants, she thought.

The living room served as the Witch's business office. Its most functional piece of furniture was a couch that opened into a bed. She did not sleep here, but on a smaller bed in a smaller room where customers were not allowed. With a pull of her hand she set loose the whore bed. The wonder of it: a couch that held a bed, a bed that held a couch. *A woman bears a child, the child consumes the woman that bore her and grows into that selfsame woman. The woman consumes the child that she has been and bears the child she will be, and so on, down through the ages.*

She stripped off her underwear and stood for a moment before the mirror. Her breasts were too large, too low slung to be fashionable these days, but she was proud of them; in their sensitivity and plenty, they had served man and child alike.

She put her hair up and took a short tub bath (Aronson liked it clean), and roughly toweled herself dry. The moment had arrived for work lace—black bra, purple stockings, black high-heeled shoes, garter belt, no underpants, the feast Aronson had ordered.

For some men she paraded in Queen of Sheba outfits, wild jungle stuff. To these fellows, sex was not exactly a human activity. They pretended they were animals, the better to forget they were men. Some liked her to dress in frilly undies and petticoats and play the scared virgin. She guessed these souls harbored secret desires to bed their sisters or daughters. Garter belts and stockings were especially popular among her clientele. She reckoned such rigs represented harnesses, harking

46

back perhaps to a time when men, lonely on the range, loved their beasts of burden as if they were women, later to return home to make the women they loved into beasts of burden.

She checked her outfit in the full-length mirror. "I wear black only for work and funerals," she said to the mirror. She didn't see her body now; she saw equipment to operate her business, and she scrutinized it as such. Did it look the way it was supposed to? Would it do the job it was designed for? What could be done to improve it? Too bad she couldn't get spare parts for it. The mirror told her the equipment was sufficient for the task at hand, at least as required by Aronson and her other old men. She was pleased, her pride the pride of the workman for his made thing.

She pulled the chair before the mirror. Beside her on an end table she placed a pan of water, a washcloth, a piece of kitchen sponge, and some tissue; on her lap was a makeup kit. It resembled an artist's paint box, with brushes, tubes, trays, and compartments for holding tins of colored powder. Staring, almost startled, into the mirror, as if seeing not herself but some creature from the beyond, she touched her face, gently at first, then more vigorously; she stroked it, kneaded it, hurt it to bring the blood to it. Soon she was seeing it: her face. Whatever changes she made, underneath would be this: skin only her hands had touched, a face only her eyes had seen.

She opened the makeup kit, and with that act her idea of self, the dear self, began to fog over. Her face would not be seen. It would disappear. What would be seen would be a mask. *I create a mask and call it a face. I am the Witch. I cannot be pleased, I cannot be injured; I can only be created, destroyed, and created again.* If she was marooned, alone, there would be no Witch because there would be no need for a witch. The Witch was the cosmetic over the true person, protecting the true person, destroying the true person. It's not just me—it's them out there. They make masks until they don't know who

47

they are underneath. *I know who I am, I am the mask, I am the Witch.*

She scrubbed her face anew with the washcloth, to disturb the skin, open the pores, make them containers. When her face was dry and tingling she applied moisturizer with her fingertips, letting the cream soak in, feeling the soft caress of it, the pleasure heightened by the contrast of the still-felt discomfort of the scrubbing.

She thought about Oliver, her mother's brother, who had taken her from her family and ripped away her girlhood. Oliver would slap her for no reason sometimes, call her names, threaten to kill her as he wept with rage, then a few minutes later apologize, speak softly to her, stroke her throat as if it were a kitten's. And they would make love, if that's what it was. She'd swoon with security, warmth, comfort. Had she brought on the violent moments for the tender ones? She didn't know. One thing was certain: without violence there was no tenderness in Oliver.

She applied the makeup with the broken piece of sponge. She dabbed it in one of the trays of color, then patted it onto her skin, smoothing it with her index finger. When she finished the first application with the sponge, the skin was dull beige, unwholesome-looking and spooky, like a mummy's buried for a couple thousand years in sand and only recently revealed by the wind. Amused by this preface to a mask, the Witch imagined herself displaying it in public arenas: the whore parading herself half-made-up in a shoe store, a funeral parlor, a restaurant, posing at the bacon bits dish of the salad bar. Note this face. See? Not alive, not dead.

She powdered in red on her cheeks; she pasted on false eyelashes; she pressed in purple mascara. Mascara: she liked the word; it was a container for "mask" and "make," and the "ah" sound at the end pleased her ears because it seemed to have a female quality.

The last task was to enhance her mouth, make it resemble a vagina. She followed its contours with bright red lipstick, leaving it glossy as a plastic flower. Suddenly everything speeded up: her heartbeat, her thoughts, her very notion of time. *Shiny and dark is the dream. Look at my lips—they suck the dream. I am the fruit of the tree. Give a nickel and taste me. Plunge into me and drown, plunge into me and consume me and be consumed by me. Plunge into me, die, and live again.* She was finished, and she inspected her creation in the mirror. It pleased her. She was pure whore now, pure Witch, perfect conjurer. There was no sign of her face.

She didn't answer Aronson's knock. She parked herself in the chair, allowed a knee to show through the robe she'd thrown on, and said, "The door is open."

He was a small-boned, fair-skinned man, shallow in the chest but with a beer gut, big ears, shifty eyes behind glasses, and a mouth on the verge of motoring even when it was still. He wasn't very tall, but his arms were long and his joints knobby, so that he seemed to be all knees and elbows. He reminded her of a small hardwood tree after its leaves have fallen. She escorted him to the living room.

"I feel like candlelight tonight," he said.

"Ain't we the romantic one," the Witch said. Usually Aronson liked his sex by moonglow. She fetched a candle, and they went into the living room. She lit a match, melted some wax on the end table beside the whore's bed, and planted the butt of the candle in the puddle before lighting it. Aronson began to undress, humming a tune, "Swanee River." The candle cast huge shadows that made her thrill just a little.

"I like that—nice light burning so bright," Aronson said. He stripped as unselfconsciously as one preparing for a solitary bath.

She let the robe slip from her shoulders and fall to the floor.

She was rather proud of that gesture, but Aronson didn't notice. He was thinking, she could see, of the story he would tell while she gave him oral sex. And he was still humming.

She watched him in the candlelight, naked except for his shoes and socks, and the shoulder holster and gun. He owned a sporting-goods store, and gun shops (he said) were favorite targets of thieves, so he had a license to carry a pistol. The dark leather, the black straps that wound over his shoulder and around his chest, the gun itself—they gave Aronson's measly body distinction.

Customer and whore stood facing each another. She took his prick between thumb and forefinger and slid her tongue under the leather of the holster until it met metal. She liked the smell of the leather and gun oil, but the metal was cold and the taste unnatural. She let go of his prick, stepped back, and eyed the gun as if it were an important person.

"You pack that everywhere you go—weddings and funerals and on the can?" she asked.

"I'm comfortable with it. It's part of me."

"Would you use it?"

He liked that question, she could see. It gave him an excuse to pull the start-up cord to his motor mouth.

"If I had to I would," he said. "I was in the artillery in the war, and never shot a personal piece at another human being. But I think, pretty much, yah, I'd use deadly force if it was called for. Because you have to with these things. It's what they're for: dispatching. Once you make the decision to carry a gun, it has to be all the way."

They stood nose to nose now and he was feeling her up. He didn't like her to put her arms around him or anything like that. He liked her to stand stock-still, with her hands by her sides.

"You in the market for a sidearm?" he asked.

"Maybe," she said. "Some kid follows me in a car."

50

"Listen, everybody needs protection today, especially a woman, and especially a woman in your line of work." He knelt and began to nibble at her pubic hairs, but kept right on talking.

"Look at it this way," he said. "Mentally a woman can be tough—I'll grant that. But physically a woman, generally speaking, is not equal to a man. But if a woman carries iron on her person, the man is not equal to her. Suppose he also carries iron? Why, then, both parties are equally weighted, and both parties are equals, are they not? And isn't that what it's all about today—dead equality among the sexes? Right? Tell me I'm wrong."

"There's something in what you say," the Witch said.

Aronson withdrew from her and stood, wiping his mouth with the back of his hand. He paced in and out of the shadows, the white of his body like the belly of a fish. And then he pulled the gun. It took all the witchness in her to stand her ground.

"This is what you need, a double-action, .38-caliber revolver," Aronson said; he was becoming aroused. "Some of these gun dealers will try to sell a woman a .22, but unless you're good with it, it may or may not shut the door on some guy's intentions. Even if you hit the sweet spot, the guy can walk right through it and stick a knife between your ribs, and you won't have the satisfaction of seeing him die five minutes later. A .38 at close range will stop him in his tracks, first time you pull the trigger. The shock alone will knock him on his ass."

"How much?" asked the Witch.

"How about I take it out in trade?" Aronson was almost erect now.

"I'll think about it," the Witch said.

"Think about it and feel it." Aronson placed the gun in her hand. It was cold. She turned the gun over and over, feeling its ridges, its indentations, smelling its oil on her fingers.

"Cold—iron-cold." She gave the gun back to Aronson.

"Actually, it's steel," Aronson said.

The Witch ignored this technicality. "I've seen enough iron in my day," she said. "Iron can only draw the warmth from a woman, and a woman cold is no woman at all."

"What are you saying?"

"No deal."

Aronson sat on the edge of the bed, and the Witch knelt before him. The candlelight was like a wind blowing shadow waves that rippled across his loins. The Witch took her teeth out and went to work. Aronson sighed.

Afterward, Aronson said, "Candlelight is so pretty. Someday when I'm in the mood for something different, I'm going to watch you ride that candle."

"Specials cost more."

Aronson didn't like that comment. It returned him to the world, its despairing hardness. "Everybody's so greedy today," he said, and impulsively he blew out the candle and snapped on the light.

The sudden brilliance, the clarity it brought, startled them both. They saw each other as if for the first time, clearly and really, she with the loosening skin and pendulous breasts, he with the matted chest hairs and slabs of fat across his middle. Their eyes met, and turned away, shamed as adolescents who have gone too far with love. Aronson reached for his pants, the Witch for her robe, until all was as it had been before the light revealed them.

Aronson paid for his pleasure and left. The Witch listened through the open window to the night carrying the sounds of his footfalls and humming. "Way down upon the Swanee River"—she whisper-sang a line from the song.

The Witch stripped the sheets and pillowcases from the whore's bed and folded it back into a couch. In the bathroom, she washed the makeup from her face. Amazing that what was so colorful on the face was so dirty on the washcloth. She took off the Witch's black lace and put on fresh cotton underpants and a cotton nightgown. She could feel the Witch in herself give way. She could be hurt now, and yet that very knowledge, the shiver of fear it sent through her, made her feel more alive, more human and noble.

She breathed in the fragrance of her tiny bedroom—powders, roses in a glass vase (that made her think of a picture she'd seen of a naked child playing a flute), and an essence she recognized as belonging to her dear self, Estelle. The room was thick with bunches of dried grass, herbs, leaves, and weeds whose names she did not know. They were pinned to the walls, hung from the ceiling, and tacked to the furniture. Spores rained down in a deluge. She swept them up, marveling at their beauty, variety, and potential.

Then she sat on her bed, her hands in her lap. With her head bowed, she resembled one about to say her prayers. As it was, the room itself was her prayer, except she had no god to offer that prayer to.

Estelle's bed was small, a child's bed almost, a bed of olden times when people were smaller, or perhaps a bed made for one woman-sized person only, a bed of wood, dry and darkened by age, but softened too, yet still strong, and made with careful attention to detail and designed to be in harmony with itself, formed by gentle hands and an idea of order by, say, a man for his convalescent mother. It was a bed that held out no invitation for company, but neither did it scorn. It was simply a bed for one.

She lay down, curled on her side. She shut her eyes, knowing sleep would not come right away. Who would visit her tonight—one of her children, Romaine, a stranger? As she wondered, the image of Oliver appeared in her mind. She dipped into her memory and plucked out a few moments in time.

"You stepped out on me when I was gone." Oliver smiled mirthlessly at her.

"Why should I? You're so great in the sack, I was satisfied just thinking about it."

"You like to scorn a man." His voice was cold and she knew he was getting ready to strike her.

"You taught me about scorn."

Oliver had managed both her personal and professional life. It was a case of the blind adult leading the blind child. He was father to her, brother, lover, and business manager. He was at his worst when he felt the crush of love for her, for love opened his eyes to the evil he had done her. Full of love, he could no longer lie to himself. He'd want to flee, but he couldn't. As he had captured her, she had captured him. So he'd drink, and find something to blame her for. Usually, infidelity. For her part, she would make sure he had good grounds for his accusations. She was unfaithful to him for the very reason that he needed her to be unfaithful.

"You went out with Junior Joyle—I know, I was told," he said.

"I didn't do nothing."

He read the lie in her eyes, and the beating began.

She summoned the feelings of that beating: the shock (no fear, but a gulping, like being taken off-guard by unexpected bad news), the sting of a hand cracking across her face (not so bad), the spinning (horrible), the *uh!* of his breathing (that reminded her of herself in child labor), the nausea, and, finally, all the feelings turned inside out into a terrible tenderness.

And he was kissing her throat, forcing himself into her. It always ended that way, with lust.

Afterward, he wiped her brow with his fingertips and watched her weep softly.

Oliver might have consumed her in the bright fires of his violence, thus giving her what she'd wanted all along, and what—now, in her bed—she still wanted, a final plunge into light. The wrongness of their love, the mere bad luck of two people bad for each other, would have died with her. But they'd had a child, almost as if she'd meant to guarantee that the wrongness of their love would be carried into the future to create a greater wrong, as if she'd meant to perpetuate the kinship as she scarred it. Their son Ollie had murdered Oliver, bashing his head against a stone wall in a slow, boozy death dance, and thus had saved her from Oliver and saved his own son, Willow, by her, and she had lived on, but changed, Witch-born out of the ashes of her grief. And Ollie had died and Willow had died. It was said in the kinship that Ollie and Willow had merged into one creature and prowled the forest, but she knew better. She had seen them—blue jewels frozen by the touch of her mother love. And now the Witch herself was dying, consumed by her own conjuring. How could she, Estelle, live on? Estelle had no answer.

She could hear the wind picking up now, shushing against the maple tree beside the auction barn. Out West, Kansas or someplace, there were, it was said, great rolling fields of golden wheat, no trees in the way to break up the view, no hogback mountains to discourage the eye yearning to see far away, no twisting roads to remind one of bad memories, just miles and miles of wheat bending in the wind, the sound of the wind on that bended wheat (that she had heard only in her imagination) like a mother whispering to her child, "Hush, hush, hush," perhaps the sound of the wind startled now and then by a swoop of birds, up and over, then back into, the wheat. With this, the thought blossoming into an image, Estelle put herself to sleep.

6

Back-of-the-Barn
Adult Books 'n' Flicks

Headed east on his first trip to Boston, Critter proceeded under a false sense of security provided by his van. Driving it made him feel protected, smarter than the average Jordan, enclosed by a second skull. The presence of Crowbar also conspired to make him believe all was well. The dog was first-rate company, obedient, even-tempered, big, comforting to have around as a loaded gun.

"I wish Ike could see us now." Critter addressed the dog.

Crowbar, watching the highway from the passenger seat, nodded agreeably.

The fact was, Critter had mixed feelings about his father's ghost. He wished Ike really could see him now, a success in the business Ike had started; but he was also happy Ike was dead and buried. Ike had had a way of keeping him suspended between his boyhood and his Jordan manhood. With Ike's death, Critter had been overwhelmed not by grief but by relief. The hurt of his father's passing had been like the hurt of sunlight to the prisoner released from his dark cell.

Critter had put reins on Ike's untamed enterprises and corralled them. The first need had been to pay debts. Critter had solved this problem by liquidating Ike's auction business. It had been a pleasure to sell the things Ike had gathered over a lifetime, a pleasure to kiss the auctioneering life good-bye.

How sick it had made Critter to watch Ike deceive grieving widows for the spoils of a house suddenly too big, too full, how disturbing to transport from house to auction barn the belongings of the recently deceased, the smell of the dead man still alive in his things.

The second need had been to straighten out Ike's property holdings. If there was one lesson he'd learned from Ike it was how to gaff a crew, so he'd rounded him some kin and fixed the run-down houses Ike owned in Tuckerman and sold them off. That gave him a power in the kinship, endeared him to the bankers Ike had alienated, and gave him some capital to concentrate on his efforts in Darby Depot. He sold off some places, bought others. He paneled, painted, and raised rents. He converted village houses into apartment units. As he had said to Delphina, "So many people get divorced today, they need more places to live." He'd been right; the apartments were always full. He had half a hope that one day local people would refer to him as the Squire of Darby Depot, as they continued to refer to Reggie Salmon as the Squire of Upper Darby even though Salmon had died. At the moment, Critter was even-steven with the banks. Soon he might creep ahead. He envisioned the day he would be the first genuinely rich Jordan.

Critter had been able to gain control of Ike's estate because Ike had left no will and never bothered to marry Elvira, the woman he had lived with after Critter's mother had deserted the family. Critter had been Ike's only legitimate heir. On behalf of herself and her children by Ike, Elvira might have contested Critter's takeover and, Critter had heard, she had been so advised by a social worker. But she was not a woman of much iron (weak was how Ike preferred his loved ones), and Critter had averted trouble by offering her the succor of a house with free rent. Still, he worried some about his half-brothers, Andre and Alsace. He would have to keep his eye on them.

A car whizzed by and Critter caught a glimpse of a woman's blond hair. In his imagination, he quickly constructed a face and body to go with the hair. Here he dwelled for a few minutes, until the image, flimsy to begin with, fell apart into a mess of color and shapes, like a tissue blown out in a hard sneeze. He remembered, then, his mission: to Boston and the Combat Zone.

"Well, Crowbar, sometimes the bear puts his foot in the trap so he can show himself he can without springing it."

Crowbar yawned aloud.

Critter had remained faithful to Delphina. For one thing, if he cheated on Delphina he knew he would have to lie to her. Ike's power had been in his ability to lie, and therefore Critter was uneasy with deception, unless it was the offhand kind of lie you told for sport or in service of a dollar. Also, he was afraid of bringing home a social disease. Also, there was the nature of his sexuality, the keep of his private self. When he only thought about sex, he was frustrated; when he only did it, he was disappointed. In order to feel comfortable, whole, rounded—fulfilled by sex—he had to think about it and do it at the same time. The problem was he couldn't think about the woman he was doing it with while he was doing it with her. It didn't matter whether he was doing it with Del or somebody else, he would be thinking about yet another person. What he needed was not somebody else to bed down, but more somebody elses to think about bedding down.

"Mr. Bach in the Combat Zone will help us rectify this situation, eh, Crowbar?"

Crowbar gurgled, sounding like a dog practicing its growl.

Critter had devised a plan both to satisfy his private self and to make the auction barn pay. He would open an adult bookstore in the rear of the barn. The purpose of his trip to Boston was to complete a deal for books, magazines, films, and peepshow equipment.

His confidence held until the van came over a rise on Route 2. Below, fifteen or twenty miles away, loomed the cityscape squatting in pale, dirty reddish-yellow light, a jumble of buildings, bridges, and vague shapes that for all he knew might have been ships or dragons, but certainly not anything from the world as he understood it. The light itself, hazy from pollution, seemed strange and unearthly to him.

"It's like they blew up an A-bomb," he said.

Crowbar barked in concurrence.

The city was immense, imposing, unreal, as if a nightmare had flashed from his mind onto a giant drive-in movie screen. He dived into a burrow of memory: himself home in the backyard, smoking a cigarette, drinking a beer, casually tending to a steak on the grill, Ollie and Jawj playing but behaving and in sight, Del in the kitchen mooshing potatoes for a salad. That helped a little to file the edges of his panic, which he recognized as the ancient Jordan fear of leaving Tuckerman County. He had first sensed the panic in Ike (an acid smell from his body) and then in himself during trips he and his father made to Connecticut to fence certain stolen items. He couldn't say whether Ike passed down the feeling to him, or whether it was in him to begin with, like an allergy, ready to rub his nerves raw at every weak moment outside the county. He had thought he had outgrown the feeling. Now he was reminded a man never outgrows anything. Prod a man in the right place and you can bring to the surface his every thought, word, deed, and blood memory.

"The blue door beside the Silk Stocking Lounge in the Combat Zone." Those had been Mr. Bach's directions, and Critter had no doubt he'd find the Silk Stocking Lounge, but where was the Combat Zone? All he knew was it was the hootchy-kootchy district—bars, bright lights, sluts, guys playing pocket pool.

"Ike's in hell laughing at me." He whispered to himself so

59

the dog wouldn't hear the frailty in his voice, but Crowbar did hear—and cringed. Critter hadn't intended to hit Crowbar, but since the dog was asking for it, he obliged, smacking him on the ear. He felt better then, but not much. Here in Massachusetts he was no longer the successful young businessman from New Hampshire. He was just another Jordan hick, full of panic at having wandered too far beyond the borders of home.

Coming into the city, he was overwhelmed by the rows upon rows of dark, gloomy buildings, lacking not only yards but even space between them. Surely people didn't work or live in such forbidding environments. Increasing his anxiety were the roads, which went every which-a-way, and the traffic, which progressed in a distinctly hostile manner, as if every driver had a grudge against every other driver.

The buildings got higher and higher as he drove deeper and deeper into the city. Then there was the river. He hadn't expected a river. He saw sailing vessels, operated by people who hung their bottoms over the high sides of their crafts; he saw men oaring excessively long, skinny boats. Why? Why in the world would anyone want to row a boat when you could put a motor on it? Men and women jogged along the sidewalk by the river. Who were they? Where were they going? And why in the world was everybody and everything all bunched up? What was a city, if not topography gone mad?

It popped into his head that the joggers and the boaters and the motorists also were going to see Mr. Bach in the Combat Zone. Although he knew this notion to be unsound, it brought him a small comfort, and there for a few minutes he camped. He imagined a line winding for miles, people waiting, like himself, to purchase dirty books and films. Perhaps if he followed a car, any car, it might lead him to the Combat Zone, or if not there, at least somewhere. Somewhere was better than nowhere. A taxi passed him. Critter took this as a sign.

A taxi driver knew where he was going. He would follow the taxi. It would take him to the Combat Zone. An image came to mind from television: Louie, the short, stocky dispatcher on the program *Taxi*. Mr. Bach would resemble Louie, his head-quarters like the taxi depot in the television show. Mr. Bach would be a dispatcher not for taxis but for UPS-style trucks lugging dirty books. Meanwhile, a voice drummed in his head, "Unsound idea, unsound idea, unsound idea."

The taxi turned off the four-lane road onto a regular city street, and although he knew better, Critter followed. Traffic slowed. They approached a great big park, a village common exaggerated to satisfy the vanity of a city. This was better, not so rush-rush. Soon the taxi turned onto another street, but Critter did not follow. He was beginning to come around in himself. He wasn't going to find Mr. Bach by motoring along the streets of Boston. This wasn't a two-road town or even a five-road town. This was a big city, *the* big city of New England. He was going to have to park the van and ask directions. He drove around the common twice, getting calmer and calmer. Maybe it was the green grass and the trees in the park, but soon he was himself again, confident, happy in the fact of who he was.

There was no place to pull over. All these people in Boston weren't headed for the Combat Zone, they were looking for a place to park. Just when the panic was on the verge of re-turning, Critter spotted a sign—PARK. Minutes later he found himself in a huge cellar, on the second tier of a downtown Boston parking garage. By the time his eyes got used to the gloom of the cellar, he'd climbed some cement stairs and he was outdoors again in the bright of the day, standing on green grass, on the common. He paused for a moment, concentrating on the feel of the soles of his feet, better to put him in touch with what he knew to be below. All those cars underfoot—amazing, incredible, mind-boggling.

Crowbar at his side, he began to walk along a wide footpath. He studied the faces of the people he passed. They all carried a certain look that detached them from other people. Critter knew the look well. After generations of living in crowded shacks and crowded apartment houses, every Jordan had mastered the ability to detach himself from the din of humanity and to project a look that said, I am pretending I am alone, don't tread on me. The difference was this was the first time Critter had seen the look on the faces of people out of doors.

He began to take in the offerings of the city—people of different colors, people dressed for weddings and people dressed in the only clothes they owned, gangs of youths, lone teenagers with mobile music boxes, daffy old women dragging plastic garbage bags, men with briefcases, men and women alike lonely as mountains, and a constant flow of pretty girls, who made him want to sing and dance but who also made him wistful because he would never see them again.

"Boston ain't so bad," he said.

Crowbar yawned an uh-huh.

He watched a cop standing on a street corner look up into the sky as if that was where he wished to be. Critter said, "Where's the Combat Zone?"

The cop frowned at Crowbar, and said, "Where in the Combat Zone do you want to go?"

"The Silk Stocking," Critter said.

It was only a short walk to the Combat Zone. Here fewer people strolled. The streets were dirtier, the red-brick buildings struck Critter as stunted. Although it was not yet noon, a few prostitutes prowled the streets. They looked like prostitutes to Critter because they wore miniskirts and mesh stockings. Guys walked with stiff necks. Here and there bums lurched. A man lay curled in an overcoat in an alleyway. Critter, curious, bent to look at his face. The man's eyes were glazed over from booze or drugs or illness, maybe all three, and he had a stubble of beard that seemed permanent. Except for the fact that the man was black, he looked for all the world like any Jordan down on his luck.

"Wonder who these fellas go to for succor?" Critter said aloud, and for once didn't care that Crowbar did not respond.

The place seemed almost familiar, as if he'd lived here in some previous lifetime. Critter felt right at home in the Combat Zone.

The Silk Stocking was inviting. Lettering on the walls promised girls totally nude. Critter was tempted to stop in for a drink, but he knew better than to get liquored up before doing business, nor did he want to leave Crowbar unattended on the street. So he swallowed his urges and knocked on a blue door.

Mr. Bach did not resemble Louie in the least. He was a tall, nervous man dressed in denim with slick black hair and a small gold earring. He sat at a big wooden desk stacked high with paperwork and dirty books. Critter eyed the books, Mr. Bach eyed Crowbar.

"Why do people keep these large dogs?" Mr. Bach said.

Critter made a mental note that Mr. Bach was the type to talk to you as if you weren't there. Before getting down to business, Critter figured he better do something to get some respect from Mr. Bach.

"Sit!" Critter shouted so loud that for a moment he thought Mr. Bach was going to draw a pistol. But he only flinched. Crowbar sat, tongue hanging out, and Critter knew he'd made his point with Mr. Bach.

"I deal in cash," Critter said.

"Well, well," Mr. Bach said.

They worked out the details, step by step. Critter liked the way Mr. Bach did business, cut-and-dried, no fooling around, no papers to sign, strictly cash-and-carry.

"You ship to me?" Critter asked.

"We can—customer's cost."

"How about I pick up the stock myself, periodically in my van?"

"Fine—no problem," Mr. Bach said. "Once a month, once every three months—whatever. The customer, him and me count everything together. One, two, three. They pay me, they load it. Everybody's happy."

"Suppose I run low, or there's something in particular I need."

"If they want some specialty items, telephone in the order, and we'll ship it."

"UPS?"

"Whatever."

Afterward, Mr. Bach didn't shake hands. That suited Critter fine.

The Witch was on the alert from the moment Critter arrived at the auction barn with kin, the four of them wearing carpenter aprons and carrying tools. Like people everywhere who lived in buildings owned by others, she associated workmen with trouble. Workmen meant change; change meant improvements, which meant higher rents; change meant expansion, which meant more folk in the building; change meant demolition, which meant eviction. They were going to do something to the barn, her home. The arrival of workmen loosed upon the Witch a score of memories of packing up, begging or borrowing a truck from kin (and the resulting loss of ascendancy); of tramping across the country to look at this or that swillhole for shelter, of becoming alternately excited and depressed by apartment ads in the newspaper, of feeling that peculiar and unique *whump* of air that only a door slammed in your face can produce, of being lied to and of having to lie—Yes, I'm married; my husband's at the shop at this very minute. No, we don't have no kids—wouldn't have 'em around. No, we don't have no pets—hate 'em. We like a neat place and quiet.

From the balcony of her apartment she watched her kins-
men below in the barn—Critter, his teen-age half-brothers
Andre and Alsace, their uncle Abenaki. She heard swear words
from Critter, an exclamation of denial from Alsace, a cackle
from Abenaki. Then laughter all around. They moved, and
now the barn air carried their voices to her.

"I don't believe I've ever seen a carpenter's apron quite so
distinguished," Critter teased Abenaki.

"'Distinguished'—Critter, you certainly have put some gravy
in your vocabulary," mocked Andre.

"'Quite so dinstinguished.'" Alsace always tried to do his
older brother one better, and always came out second best.

"It ain't distinguished, it's dirty—dirty with blood—and I
love it," Abenaki said. He was short, brick-hard in the gut,
bow-legged, and nimble. He lived in a shack in the woods,
usually alone, but recently he had offered succor to Andre and
Alsace. Abenaki was oddly vain. He wore the camouflage outfit
of the bow hunter as a daily uniform. His dark hair fell to his
shoulders. He never washed it but combed it frequently; it
shined from its own oils. He trimmed his beard so it came to
a point three inches below his chin.

"You shooting animals out of season again?" Andre pretended to scold Abenaki.

"I know what he done—I seen him," Alsace said.

Abenaki cuffed Alsace. The brothers laughed, except for
Critter.

"Blood? You slaughter some game?" Critter needed to clear
up in his mind the matter of the bloody apron.

"No slaughter, an operation. Castrated a pig. Took the mean-
ness right out of him," Abenaki said.

"Tell brother Critter what you ate for supper that night,"
Andre said, and he and Alsace hee-hawed like mad fools.

"Tasty—tasty," Abenaki cackled.

"Let's get to work," Critter said.

The Witch eased down the steep wooden steps to the main floor of the barn. When Critter was alone, standing on a ladder, nails in his mouth, the Witch confronted him.

"Remodeling?" she prodded.

"Umm." He had seen her out of the corner of his eye, and been careful not to look in her direction.

"Coming along pretty good."

"Umm."

He was such a handsome fellow in his white overalls, a nice, big boy, full of pep and big ideas.

"Critter!" Her voice, charged with command, was not without affection.

"Umm."

"Get the metal out of your mouth. The Witch has something to say to you."

Critter spilled the nails into his palm. A few fell to the floor. The Witch picked them up, and handed them to Critter.

"This is my home," she said.

"I know."

The Witch folded her arms, and turned her head away from him. The gesture compelled Critter to tell her about his plans.

"An adult bookstore—what should I think about that?" the Witch said, and scorned Critter with a laugh.

"Don't think nothing about it. It don't concern you." Critter's feelings were hurt. That was a good sign. It showed Critter could be pushed and pulled this way or that.

"'Course it concerns me," the Witch said, deliberately sounding as if she were trying to explain something to a child. "What hours you plan to keep? You going to put lights on to bother these old eyes? You going to play loud music in the middle of the night? What kind of a crowd is an adult bookstore going to attract?"

"We'll be open three to eleven at night to start with. Except

Sunday—town's got an ordinance about business on Sunday. Can't do it unless you sell food."

"Oh, Critter, ain't you law-abiding." The Witch was enjoying herself.

"This establishment won't bother you none, Witch. It'll be around back, and you won't see no lights, and I got a little manager to take care of the place."

That got the Witch's attention. "What you mean—you have a little manager?"

"I thought I'd hire a woman," Critter said. "Men like to look at a skirt and, well..."

"And, well, you can get 'em cheap."

"That, too," Critter said, a little less on the defensive, a little more put out. "You could've had the job. I offered it to you. So, I had to go looking, but I hit it lucky. Noreen Cook is going to be my manager."

The Witch reeled inside as if socked in the stomach. "Noreen!" she shouted. "Noreen can't manage her period."

The work went on. Trucks rolled from the highway down the long dirt drive carrying sheets of plywood, lumber, gypsum board, window casings, wire, insulation. Sometimes materials arrived in huge cardboard boxes, and the mystery of what might be in them captured the Witch's imagination. Sex gadgets—they got sex gadgets in there, she thought. She had no clear picture in her mind what these might be, diddly-doos and such, but she could be pretty sure they were invented and manufactured by cunning Asians and beyond the ken of a poor country whore. She was curious and jealous and a little stirred.

Her apartment was at one end of the auction barn and the entry to the store was around the back of the barn, out of sight both from her landing and the highway. However, from her balcony on the inside of the barn, she could watch the men

67

frame in and, finally, panel off her view. The project reduced the space for the weekend flea market by a third, but that didn't matter much because there was still room enough for the dozen or so vendors. The Witch noted a back door connecting a storage room in the store with the interior of the barn.

The work went fast, ending with the implantation of a sign at the head of the driveway, a magnificent sign, the Witch had to admit. It was tall and stately, well lighted at night, with a drawing of a dancing girl in a G-string like one the Witch herself once wore at a private party, the lettering on the cream background in three tiers, the top and bottom tiers in black, the middle in red:

BACK-OF-THE-BARN
ADULT
BOOKS 'N' FLICKS

Next day the store opened. The Witch was on the lookout; she counted only five customers. But business picked up in the weeks that followed. Cars seemed to come and go willy-nilly. A fellow would drive hesitatingly into the lot early in the morning, and when he found the store unopen he'd peel out. What the Witch heard was not the sound of the car's tires but the sound of a man's anger, a sound that felt like an approaching argument with a loved one. She was at once repelled and attracted by the feeling. In the same way, the bookstore itself disturbed her while it freshened her. The bookstore was like the Trans Am in that it held out the possibility of terror; in terror, the experience of it, immersion in it, the Witch recognized a medium for transformation.

Noreen accepted the wooden pot of dried weeds the Witch brought her.

"For me? I don't believe it," she said. "Nobody brings me nothing. Did you get them in the mall?"

She was wearing a red dress, decorated in black across the front with the phrase BACK-OF-THE-BARN, the letters distorted somewhat as they snaked over her small breasts.

"I most generally swap for the pots, but the dried weeds I pick myself," the Witch said, while the thought in her mind was, The dear self picks those weeds.

"Weeds," Noreen said, as if searching for meaning by uttering the word.

"When the green goes out of a plant, and it gets brittle and creaks when the wind blows, that's when I pick it. Protect it, then, and it lasts forever. The green stuff is nothing, a trick that eventually rots, stinks, and disappears. The dry stuff is tough to find this time of year, for the green, but it's there and it lasts."

"Is that so?" Noreen said, in awe, uncomprehending. She put the pot on the cash register on the counter, which rested on a raised platform two steps above the floor of the bookstore. Noreen sat on a stool behind the register. The Witch remained standing on the main floor, content to be at the lower level.

"Do you put them in water?" Noreen asked.

She has a beautiful face that doesn't know anything, the Witch thought. Maybe that's why it's beautiful.

"You don't put anything that's dried in water," the Witch said, a hint of malice in her voice.

"I guess I knew that," Noreen said, ashamed, but not sure exactly why. "I thought maybe if you put them in water, the green would come back."

"If you had the wherewithal, Noreen, you'd stand and cheer and say, 'I'm for everything green and everybody happy,' wouldn't you, now?"

"I suppose I would," Noreen said, uncertain whether the Witch was mocking her or not.

The Witch turned abruptly away from Noreen. She pretended to stroll about, but she hardly saw the racks of magazines, the peep-show booths. She had retreated into herself. *Noreen is very clever, Noreen is trying to take advantage of me, Noreen is completely innocent, Noreen is the blush on an apple.* What to make of Noreen, what to make of herself contemplating Noreen—the Witch didn't know. All she had to guide her were her feelings: strong, compelling, confusing— half grief, half desire: the tremor.

"This place tire you?" the Witch asked, in an attempt to ground herself in the trivial.

"The hours are long, and I get lonely," Noreen said. "The men that come in here, they're not like people. They don't look at you or they look at you like... you know. But I'm not complaining. It's not so hard on your feet as waitressing, and there's long periods when I can just sit here and daydream. Who can complain about a job where you get paid for daydreaming? I try to keep busy. I sweep the floor and wipe the benches in the booths, and put the magazines back in the right place. But I don't fix projectors when they break. I give the customer his token back. Then I call Critter and he fixes the machines. He's here maybe five times a week. He does inventory and he tells me about his plans. Then it's not so lonely."

Having found in Noreen's words the triviality she sought, the Witch was disgusted, enraged by it; she felt betrayed.

"You had a hard life, a hard childhood?" The Witch pinned Noreen with her eyes.

"I don't like to think about it."

"You don't think about much, do you?"

"If I thought about my life, I'd probably kill myself." Noreen was near tears.

The Witch's anger with Noreen fizzled as quickly as it had flamed.

"You do well not to think." The Witch's voice was tender now. "Myself, I think too much; worse, you see, I conjure. I know the life you've had, because I've lived it: a womanhood awakened early and the men there to take advantage, shake their heads at one another and agree whatever happened was your fault. A boozehound for a father, a mother weighed down with other children, fear, and maybe health problems. Always choosing the wrong man, always laboring in the wrong ways to hold him because you don't know no better."

"I'm still here, I'm still alive." Noreen shook her tiny fist. She had dug down and found some strength.

The Witch saw the confusion in Noreen, her sadness, and through it all her power, which was her ability to endure suffering and in that suffering to rekindle the hope suffering had consumed. It was a power Noreen herself could not see, perhaps could not appreciate even if she could see it, for her own lack of... what was it? Intelligence? Wisdom? A Witch in her soul?

"What impresses me about you, Noreen, is you're good, you don't use people; you've managed to stay out of the whore's bed." The Witch resisted an impulse to take Noreen's hand, squeeze it, crush it.

Noreen was embarrassed on the Witch's behalf. "I'm not perfect," she said. "I talk dirty now and again."

"Oh, what's that? Nothing. Everybody talks dirty today—men, women, boys, girls, parrots. Girls walk down the street like sluts even when they aren't slutting. They dress like bimbos, smoke like pool-hall bums, say *shit* out loud, and scratch their asses in public."

"That's the way things are today," Noreen sighed, as one who had never experienced how things were yesterday and didn't, at bottom, care.

As she went on, the Witch found herself first on the side of sarcasm, now on the side of sincerity, never secure on either side. "Females have acquired all the disgusting habits of males," she said. "So what? From depot to hilltop, everybody sleeps around today. You sleep around, Noreen?"

Noreen blushed.

"Don't bother to answer," the Witch said.

"I don't sleep with somebody unless it's the real thing," Noreen said, trying to set the record straight, but the Witch ignored her, steaming along with her own train of thought. "Everybody sleeps for free today and everybody gives orals to everybody else. Makes life difficult for a professional woman, believe you me. Not that I'm criticizing progress."

Noreen now was aching to say something, and her ache gave her the courage to interrupt the Witch. She blurted out, "Love—you forgot love."

The Witch drifted out of the store, realizing in the brightness of the late-afternoon sun that her mind actually hadn't registered what her eyes had seen, the hundreds of books in the store, the pictured flesh, the peep-show booths. Even the image of Noreen was unclear, bright but shattered, as if recalled from long ago. And, too, it was as if she'd been talking not to Noreen but to a ghost. She conjured Noreen by two separate lights. She could truthfully say she wanted to save Noreen from a terrible evil, even if she couldn't define the nature of that evil; at the same time, she could truthfully say she herself was that evil—that if she destroyed Noreen, she would bring herself peace of mind. Yet Noreen the person meant nothing to her. Her feelings were not for Noreen but for that ghost.

7

The Old Farmer

The Witch, returning from tending her marijuana patch, heard the excited cries of her great-grandson Ollie. Up ahead she saw Critter and his entire family—wife, kids, dog, car. They were clustered about a giant snapping turtle that had wandered into the parking lot of the auction barn. The turtle had retreated into its dark green shell, while Critter crouched beside it with a stick. He teased the turtle by waving the stick before its hidden nose. In the background, Crowbar barked, Baby Jawj howled, the Caddy's radio played pop music, and Delphina whined like a stuck record: "Stop poking that poor creature—stop poking that poor creature—stop poking that poor creature."

"You watch your daddy," Critter bragged to little Ollie. Critter had worked the stick to the lip of entry into the shell.

Delphina spotted the Witch and said to her, "He won't stop poking that poor creature."

"What do you expect? He's a Jordan," the Witch said.

"Amen," Delphina said.

Ignoring the wailing baby cradled easily in one great arm, outfitted in nothing but a yellow bikini, the top stained by huge, leaking nursing breasts, her long bleached-blond hair falling to her shoulders, her white skin sun-pinked, Delphina was an impressive sight to the Witch.

"Going to the beach?" the Witch asked.

"No such luck. Going to sit under the garden hose. Him here"—she pointed at Critter—"he don't like the water."

With that, the Witch felt the power of the kinship. She too was frightened of water. While she had never been afraid of dying, she'd always been afraid of drowning.

The turtle lunged for Critter's stick, grasping it in its powerful jaws. Little Ollie whooped in ecstasy.

"That *poor creature* will take your arm off, Del," Critter said.

He and the turtle played tug-of-war until the stick broke and Critter went flying backward onto the seat of his pants. The turtle dropped the stick and retreated into itself. Delphina's disgust flip-flopped to mirth. Ollie whooped louder. Crowbar reared up on his hind legs like a bear and yelped in amusement. Critter frowned but only for a moment before he broke out into self-mocking laughter. Even Baby Jawj got into the mood, gurgling instead of yowling. All these sounds of happiness were accompanied by the music from the Caddy's radio. This, thought the Witch, is about as close as Jordans get to joy.

In a few minutes, the family motored off, leaving the Witch with only the turtle for company. In contrast to the din of moments ago, the quiet felt oppressive, like moist heat. The turtle was still, its head, feet, and tail drawn in. Without warning, anger surged through the Witch. She picked up the stick and jabbed at the turtle a couple of times. The turtle did not respond. Her fury, the stupidity of it, struck the Witch now. She threw down the stick and stormed off.

Like some cat that had been lying in wait for its prey, the Trans Am seemed to snarl and leap out of the woods. In a moment it was not five feet behind the Subaru. The image in the car mirror, the looming road ahead, the closeness of the interior of her own car—these perceptions twisted together in her mind, obscuring for a moment the protective witch in Estelle Jordan. How little her car seemed, how delicate, how foreign. And now she was picturing a girl pedaling a bicycle in heavy automobile traffic, the girl's pink underpants showing under a flowered dress. She knew that dress yet did not know it. As a child she had stared at it in a store window for weeks until one day it was gone. Forgotten for five decades, the memory of the dress returned bright, vivid, rich in detail, unattainable as love. And she was the Witch again.

They played this game at his convenience two or three times a week; she'd watched the leaves fill out on the trees, brighten through June like new tumors, then turn dull and dusty with the yellow July sun. Something had to change.

She speeded up, slowed, turned onto Center Darby Road, turned off at River Road, speeded up, slowed. She pulled off the road where she reached the place under the trees where the Trans Am had exposed himself to her. Today the forest seemed closer, darker, the air heavier, sweeter. Without consciously deciding anything, she jammed the accelerator pedal to the floor. The rear tires kicked dirt and she was back on the road again, the Trans Am on her tail. In a moment, she broke free from the forest. The sky spoke to her: See how immense I am. The sunlight made every thing distinct from every other thing, the bright-tar road distinct from the dull-dirt shoulder, a shallow ditch distinct from a barbed-wire fence, the wavy green field distinct from the flat white sky. Her eye meandered upslope about sixty yards to a dip of land where the backhoe lay in state, mired in mud to the axle, a rust bucket of magnificent proportion and shape. It resembled a defeated beast. And with that thought, she remembered her father, hoisting her onto his shoulders to watch her mother dance on the wooden floor of a meeting house, she'd forgotten in which

town. The music that night, contredanse, played once again
in her mind. It made her feel like a child safe from the pouring
rain—oh, the tremor as music was almost unbearable.

The field crested, dipped, and ended at a stone wall and a
border of trees. Beyond was the Connecticut River, not visible
but felt, imposing and deliberate as the men who farmed along
its banks.

She slowed her car and brought it to a halt on the shoulder.
The Trans Am sped by, stopping ahead. The engines of the
two cars idled, like the breathing of boxers between rounds.
It occurred to her that she had inadvertently frustrated him,
mocked him. There was no cover. He could not risk leaving
the car fully masked for fear a passing motorist would spot
him in his gawd-awful getup. She had him penned in his car,
penned in his costume, penned in his warped mind. The Witch
found herself amused.

She stepped out of the car and stood for a moment in the
road—look at me, look at me. Cow-smell wound down upon
her—rich, fragrant, fertile. The fence posts were pleasantly
out of plumb and rotting at their bases. The black-white of the
holstein cows clashed with the green of the fields. The cows,
about twenty of them, stopped grazing and turned in stupefied
attention toward her. They looked for all the world like people
watching television.

She listened for the music of the river, hearing instead the
traffic on I-91 west of the river in Vermont. The river might
as well have dried up; the highway had become the river. There
was no music in the sounds of the interstate, but a steadfast
din that troubled her. It was like listening to the sound of
yourself breathing all the time. It could drive you crazy. Maybe
something like that had happened to Romaine.

She glanced at the Trans Am. He was watching her through
his mirror. The gleam of the mouth zipper of the mask lacerated her eye. She tiptoed across the ditch (the ground was

76

firm), lifted the top strand of the barbed wire where it had gone a little slack, and slipped under, taking it as a sign of encouragement to go on that she didn't catch her skirt. She headed for the backhoe for no better reason than it was there, impressive and upraised in a landscape that defined itself by being underfoot.

When she was halfway between the backhoe and the road, she turned and faced the Trans Am. He gunned the engine, startling her with the roar from the mufflers. This is dangerous, this is foolish, she thought. She should return to the relative safety of her car. But she remained still, immobilized by sunlight, by music—something. She bowed her head shyly, her hands awkwardly a-jitter at her sides, as if she were a child under the scrutiny of a greater power.

Her gesture of submission puffed the confidence of the Trans Am, stimulated him to act. The car backed slowly down the road until it was almost out of sight, then it stopped, huffing in place for a moment. The engine revved, its sound building from a throaty gurgle to an angry whine. She sensed the second when it was about to leap ahead, and she quickened in anticipation. At the noise of the popping of the clutch, she reached an imaginary hand inward to feel the tremor, as a lover reached outward for his partner. Smoke spat from the squealing tires, the rear end wiggled, the body bucked forward; the car laid a hundred yards of rubber on the road. Then, showing off brakes, the Trans Am came to a smooth stop. The car panted in place, shifted gears, revved, and backed slowly to the starting point. There it idled contentedly for a minute or two, preparing for the next run.

She listened to the engine, feeling her own satisfaction in its low doglike growl. She remembered herself on the front steps of a shack, listening to the highway, where teenage boys raced fast cars. The sense of sadness associated with the memory made her realize that what she was feeling now was an old woman's weak imitation of the thrill teenage girls feel when boys are showing off for them. She had never experienced the feeling in its pure form. Now, buried in the Witch's knowledge, the sensation vanished entirely, replaced by anger, betrayal, humiliation—emotions all too familiar. By the time the Trans Am finished his second run, the Witch was sickened by these feelings. The joke was on her.

"I'll get you," she whispered, threatening both the Trans Am and the dear self that had allowed this pain to surface.

The Witch threw her head up in defiance, raised her arm, and flipped out her middle finger.

The Trans Am, until now posturing triumphantly, stalled his engine. The Witch laughed. The Trans Am started with a screech, then quieted to a sullen idle. The Witch laughed louder and more theatrically so her scorn could not be mistaken. The Trans Am's engine sputtered and complained—*erninininini*.

"Get your feelings hurt?" the Witch shouted.

The Trans Am revved belligerently, and the car began to move.

The Witch stopped laughing. Her greed for the pleasure of his hurt had made her careless; she had pushed him too far. The car glided along the narrow shoulder of the road, turned off where the ditch was broad and shallow, then ripped through the fence. It headed for her, bucking and squealing and murderous, determined for blood as any long-tormented animal suddenly uncaged. The cows scattered, as well as cows can; they could see the Trans Am meant business.

The Witch understood, almost sympathized—you receive an injury, you pay it back with interest.

The only possible refuge was the backhoe. She glanced up at it. Stiff and indifferent as a god it was, and too far away to run for. Someone young and lithe, such as Noreen, might make it, but not herself. If she ran, it would give the Trans Am pleasure to chase her down, and she was determined not to give away pleasure. Nonetheless, it took an act of will for her to stand this ground. As the Trans Am bore down on her, the Witch felt the colors grow brighter, her sense of time slow.

Oh, Lordy, don't leave no tire marks on this soul. Oliver, take my hand. Speak to me, instruct me. "Be nice, be scared; they like it when the girl acts a little scared. It makes them feel like men." *Yes, Oliver, I will, yes, I will, yes. Whatever you say, Oliver. Only die. Do me a favor and die. Go back before they get you, Noreen. Fear is not the enemy, it's resignation, the signing over of your body to the whims of men and memory.*

There was no need to jump. The Trans Am veered off at the last second, traveled downslope, crashed through the fence, and tore down the road. She couldn't tell whether the Trans Am had turned away because he had seen the tractor coming or whether he had another reason—recognition that without her his own tremor could not hold.

The Witch looked over the saggy-eyed man astride the tractor chugging toward her. Like the backhoe, man and tractor were old, out of style, worn, but well made, solid as monuments. She'd never met the man, never said a word to him, but there would be no need for introductions. She knew him and he would know her. Darby was that kind of town. You might not know everyone personally, but you knew everyone's story and they knew yours. The man would be Avalon Hillary, dairy farmer of great repute in Tuckerman County, owner of the soil under her feet. Hillary was a jowly, well-jawed man whose nose and eyes were too small for his face. The eyes were blue, wise but not cunning; the hands were rough as split firewood.

The tractor halted with a jerk as Hillary cut the engine. He shifted his considerable bulk in the saddle of the tractor and with a certain reining-in caution leaned forward to speak.

"You all right?" he asked.

79

"Still game."

"Who was that and what the hell was he up to?" Hillary was irate first, puzzled second.

"Kid hot-rodding, I imagine."

"He was lowering right for you," Hillary said, hoping, it seemed to the Witch, for an explanation.

"Just a kid showing off," the Witch said.

"Goddamn 'em—pardon my French—they destroy a good fence, tear tender sod, scare the dickens out of a lady and some innocent cows, and for what?"

"For fun."

"Oh, is that it? Vandalize, trespass, frighten—all for fun; for nothing, I say." Hillary talked slowly, in anger but without rancor. He shook his head as if hearing bad news.

At first the Witch thought he honestly believed fun was nothing, but then she realized he was mourning his own incapacity for fun. She understood such men, understood their weariness, fellows who had been go-getters all their lives and now found themselves unable to keep up to the standards they had set when they were thirty, fellows wondering whether to go on with revised standards or pack it in.

Then there was an awkward moment between them because he expected her to say something, and she kept a silence.

"You, ah, like these pastures, do you?" he said.

She translated this question as a polite inquiry into her presence on his property.

"I do like to walk fields. I smell the grass and look at the flowers," she said.

"My wife loved flowers. She'd put them in a vase in the parlor."

The Witch remembered now that Hillary was recently widowed. She placed a hand on her hip. It was one of her more subtle come-hither poses.

*　　*　　*

80

Disgust in his face, a boy of about five resisted the pull of his mother's hand, halted at Estelle's table of weeds and weed pots, and asked, "What are those things?"

The mother jerked the boy along. "Nothing," she said, studiously avoiding eye contact with Estelle.

Two hours had passed since the flea market had opened at eight, but Estelle had not made a sale. It didn't matter. She had never really been at peace with herself or the world, her soul hardly knew the meaning of the word, but she knew her feeling at this moment, this Saturday-morning feeling, was close to peace, standing over her table of dried weeds and pots, watching the world go by, not the Witch, nor the dear self, but in a sort of never-never land of being.

Piper, the old gaffer who sold even older tools from the table beside her own, had seen the boy and his mother. Estelle recognized the look on his face, true concern and true vanity; it meant he was going to give her some advice.

"Estelle." He called her as one drawing the attention of a waitress, sliding a few feet closer to her, but still staying in the territory defined by his table. Like most of the other vendors, he didn't know her primary source of income. He lived in Massachusetts, a retired telephone company toll test man who'd say, bitterly, "It used to be Mother Bell, don't you know?" He made the flea-market rounds through New England in the summer, Florida in the winter.

"What's cooking?" Estelle asked. She never bothered making real conversation with Piper; he was not one to listen to a woman. Or perhaps, in this position, between selves, she wasn't capable of real conversation. She didn't know, didn't care.

"Estelle, you should wise up and make a profit for yourself," he said. "Get into videotapes or Care Bears, candleholders— anything but weeds."

She batted her eyelashes at him.

He shook his head—poor, foolish woman.

For the flea market she dressed in a plain skirt and blouse, harnessed her breasts in a bra, put her hair up, and wore a minimum of makeup. Here she could mingle with folk other than kin and clients, put the Witch in a closet for a while. Most of the vendors were from out of town, retired people mainly, pursuing their hobbies and calling them businesses. What made them intimate was the barn and the unspoken knowledge they were all imposters in that this relaxed life they lived on the weekend had nothing to do with the real, for-keeps life of weekdays. They didn't know about the Jordan Witch. She was Estelle to them.

The vendors sat on folding wooden chairs parked behind their tables. They drank coffee, munched on doughnuts, deplored the price of heating oil, exchanged stories of medical catastrophes, related anecdotes regarding their grandchildren. They talked, not toward resolution but toward relief. It was familiar talk, familiarly spoken, reminding her of the chatter around Donald's kitchen table. But there was a difference. Here she felt no strain to keep up her ascendancy within the clan. Here she could pretend she was just another body among the common run. During the best of these times she felt oddly radiant.

But there were bad moments too, when her euphoria would be turned inside out. A sense of powerlessness would sweep over her, as if she'd suddenly been set down on some vast, treeless, windswept plain. This feeling was derived in part, she understood, from the way she was treated as Estelle. When they dealt with her, the men teased her or unconsciously bossed her around, while the women used her as a sponge to sop up their complaints. More often, because she had little to say, she was ignored. As Estelle purely, she had no anecdotes to relate, no opinions to put forth, no ability to cow an aggressor, no personality to command attention. In the worst of the moments at the flea market, when she was alone, ignored, she felt precisely as she had as a child—invisible.

A middle-aged couple, she with red hair, white roots, he with lips puckered for whistling but silent, approached her table. Like most of her customers, they didn't look at her but at her things. There was something in their concentration that spoke well to her of humanity, that gave her hope. Perhaps it was that in concentrating on things, they left their pride behind.

"How much?" The woman held up the pot, looking not at Estelle but at the pot as if the pot could speak. The man leaned away from the activity, body and soul.

Estelle's optimism vanished. They were going to be typical customers. They were going to dicker.

"Five dollars for that one," Estelle said.

"Give you a dollar for it," the woman said.

"Can't pay the rent for that—four dollars and you can walk away with it," Estelle said.

"Let's go," the man said. The woman acted as if he hadn't spoken; she frowned at the pot.

Once you introduce the idea of profit, Estelle thought, people displayed their bad side. She had to fight back the impulse to give the pot to the woman.

"I can let it go for three dollars and fifty cents," Estelle said.

"It's nothing but a piece of wood with a hole in it," the man said.

The woman deepened her frown.

"I can pick a piece of wood off the yard and drill it, and it won't cost nothing," the man said, and the Witch rising up in Estelle knew that the woman would buy the pot.

In the end, she paid two dollars.

Estelle listened while Piper and the widow Kringle, who sold needlework, jawed. Piper said it wasn't good for the country to have too many millionaires. A passionately held conviction this was, but he was having difficulty presenting his arguments so they made sense. Not that this mattered. The Kringle woman nodded in agreement to everything he said. When she spoke it was about her grandson in the Navy. He was stationed in Hawaii. Didn't like it—no change in the seasons. Piper uh-huhed her, then launched another attack on big money. So it went: nodding and uh-huhing and talk whose meaning came up short. Estelle was at turns drawn and repelled by the scene, as she was by one of those lie-about-life television dramas.

She was taking a walk, getting away from her table, when she bumped into Avalon Hillary at the front door. He smelled of cow and damp field grass. The smells made her feel good—solid, connected to something, she couldn't say what.

He greeted her with a grunt of recognition.

"Starting to rain out?" she asked.

"Yes and no," he said. "I mean the sky is gray, and there's moisture in the clouds, but there isn't enough of it finding its way to the ground to do any good."

"I should have known better than to ask a farmer about the weather," she said.

Hillary laughed at himself. "That's a farmer," he said. "Never satisfied with nature. Too much rain or not enough. I can't remember a day I couldn't have improved, given a divine hand."

"I don't normally see you at this flea market," she said.

"I don't normally frequent this flea market," he said.

"Is that so?" she said.

"I'm not bragging," he said, catching the slight taint of sarcasm in her voice. "It's just there's nothing here I want."

"Nothing but company."

"You guess right into a man's innards, don't you?" he said, returning the sarcasm she had presented him.

"I don't know about that," she said.

They were moving together now, strolling like a couple at an outing. She noted he was not looking at the goods on the

84

tables but at the beams of the barn. Habit, she thought.

"I got sick of my house and my barn and my girls, the sameness maybe, and I hopped into my old Buick, said to myself, 'Avalon, why don't you go for a ride like you used to?' But I'm alone now and a ride is not the same thing as when you have somebody to talk to."

"You might listen to the radio," she teased.

"Radio music makes me suffer," he said with great exaggeration. Estelle said nothing, and the silence incited him to go on. "So I stopped here. Thought I'd look around. Impulse, I suppose."

"As you can see, not much to look at," Estelle said.

She fetched him a cup of coffee, and they talked some more. They meandered about the barn. He kept looking up at the beams.

"You know this barn?" she asked.

"More or less," he said. "Used to belong to one of the Flagg boys. When the new leg of the highway was built, it split the farm in two. Flagg didn't like the road, and he moved his house, actually trucked it away to the backside of his property. Left the barn to orphan. Left the land to orphan. Eventually sold the land. Then he sold the house. Then he sold himself out of the county. Ended up down south someplace. Town used to be full of Flaggs. Now none. Unless you count Mrs. McCurtin, who married out.... What's this door?"

"Leads to the dirty bookstore."

"Hooked up poorly, lock installed wrong—it shames this barn."

It took the Witch a moment before she realized he was not talking about the bookstore itself but about the workmanship that went into creating it.

"That's Critter," she said. Suddenly caught up in her Jordanness, she could feel the past of the kinship, serious and tragic, comical and foolish, everything the common run experienced, except more intense, more lasting for the imprint it made in the soul. She measured, as if for the first time, her correct distance from this old farmer, from Piper and the Kringle woman, from all manner of humanity outside the kinship— a million miles.

"I suppose." Avalon frowned.

"You can't bear to see something poorly constructed."

"No, ma'am—I cannot."

He stayed awhile longer, then was gone. The Witch in her reckoned it would be only a matter of time before he'd make a date with her. She figured him for a once-a-week customer, like any farmer, stingy but no crybaby; he'd probably like his sex standard, but you could never tell with a man so she reserved judgment.

Later, the afternoon winding to a close, Estelle found herself restless, uneasy. She threw a plastic sheet over her table and slunk out, not wanting to explain to the other vendors why she'd closed early. Upstairs in her apartment, sitting by a window, she smoked a bowl of toke, conjuring on her loneliness: it was like the sound and swirl of dipping oars.

Outside it was beginning to rain. A few leaves on the big maple beside the barn had turned orange. Not real, she thought, nothing more than bits of color in my eye. She saw the Trans Am then. It pulled off the highway into the drive of the auction barn. She left her apartment and walked around the corner to the parking lot. She saw the car, but not the driver. He must have gone into the bookstore. She stood in the rain, feeling its coolness on her shoulders. The car, black and silvery in the dull of the day, seemed poised to rocket off into the gloom. She hadn't seen man or car since the incident in Hillary's field a week ago. She wanted to touch the car, feel its smoothness, but something kept her off.

Half an hour went by before a young man came out of the porn shop, a paper bag under his arm. He wore a leather jacket, tight blue jeans, and black boots. His blond hair was combed rakishly from front to back; his face was smooth-shaven, perfectly chiseled, lips full. She was amazed how handsome he was. She'd never seen a face so perfect.

He didn't notice her until he was in the car leaving the lot. He had plenty of room to get by her, but he stopped. Without expression, he stared at her for a long time. Then he nudged the car slowly past her. Its subdued roar was like the purr of a big cat. When it turned onto the highway, the engine revved, the tires squealed, and the Trans Am bolted forward.

Before setting out, Avalon dressed in his suit, just as if he were going to a town meeting, and he vacuumed the mats in the Buick for no better reason than that it gave him confidence. He had never expected to pay a visit to the town pump. The idea had come out of the blue. But now that he had made the decision, he felt thrilled, free, full of energy. It was as if all the fun he'd wanted to have as a young buck was now there for the taking—his due. God was saying, "Go to it, Avalon."

The car door closed with a satisfying *thunk!* and that told him his senses were unusually keen. By gosh, he felt downright optimistic. Once on the road, rolling, he didn't have to look to know he was flanked by his land. The response of the Buick to blacktop told him. Normally, without thinking, the farmer in him would glance at his fields, looking for a broken fence, somebody's dog free, a certain lean to the trees beyond that heralded bad weather. If he couldn't fix what was rent, he'd attempt to worry it whole. Not now. Not tonight. He gave potential problems not a whit of thought. Tonight the idea of land itself was sweet, a benediction uncorrupted by work and worry, productivity and practicality. Even the sight of the backhoe, stuck in the mud, swept him, not with guilt, but with love.

* * *

She could tell right away she was going to like him in bed. He was all business. No faky romantic stuff, no quirky rules to crank him up, no talk, no bragging, no whining, no complaints about the dim lighting or the bed or her hair in the way, no stupid questions—Does the price include a shower afterward?

He was a big man, especially through the middle. But his wasn't loose fat; it was good fat, the kind you live off of. He had shaved close and she was grateful for that. He explored her, as men will the first time, with eyes, hands, lips, nuzzling her like a gentle hound. He heated up quickly for an old fart, but seemed to reach a point where he wasn't sure what to try next.

"You know what I'm famous for," she said.

"Yah."

"Want some?"

"It's been on my mind."

She took his balls in her hand, squeezed them, and dived for his pride. He lay back, relaxed, and let her work. She wondered how far he'd want her to go. Just when she thought he was ready to finish, he touched her on the shoulder. She understood the signal, and rolled over on her back. He hopped on and rode off into his sunset.

Finished, he put his arm over his eyes.

"Bet you never had any of that at home," she said.

"Maybe, maybe not," he said.

She scoffed at his attempt to keep pure the memory of his wife, or whatever prompted his evasiveness.

"Don't laugh." He neither threatened, nor begged, only asked.

"I'll laugh as I please," she said.

"Pretty haughty, you are—and show-offy," he said.

"I got the skill. Shouldn't I show it off?"

"I imagine so."

"Tell the truth now—you loved a gobble."

"It's tart, I don't deny that. Sort of like they bring you a chair to get on the hoss. But mainly, ma'am, I like it from the saddle."

"Likes it standard," she mocked him.

"Likes it standard," he returned the mockery, and they both giggled like schoolchildren.

Time passed, she wasn't sure how much. They didn't speak, but listened to one another breathe. She felt him sigh as he watched her bring the nightie across her breasts and tie a bow in the ribbon that closed it. "Get your money's worth?" she asked.

"Goddamn if I can say. I haven't done this outside of matrimony enough to know how to rate it."

"It's as good as married love. Admit that."

"Close—goddamn close."

"Can't you tell an easy lie?"

He thought about the question for a moment. "You lie a lot, do you? I mean in your line of work."

"Lie all the time."

He *umph*ed disapprovingly.

"When something goes broke on your farm, you fix it?"

"Have to."

"Me too. In my profession, lying is a valuable tool. It fixes any number of broken-down old parts."

He looked at her closely to see if she was teasing. She made sure he couldn't read an answer on her face.

He turned modestly to one side of the bed and pulled up his trousers. The Witch put on her robe. She thought that was going to be that. But he hung around, looked around, searching for an excuse not to leave. She could have offered him a cup of tea, but she wanted to see how he'd handle the situation. He eyeballed her arrangements of dried grasses, and touched a bunch carefully.

"Don't you keep any live plants?"

"I like them this way, the water gone from them," she said.

"Living plants give you allergies?"

"I'm allergic to anything alive. Makes me sad."

He didn't know how to deal with that explanation.

"Some of them, the begonias, I think, used to make my wife sneeze," he said. "Cat fur, too. So we didn't have any cats in the house. We had barn cats. They harass the rodent population. Now that she's gone, I'm thinking, I'm tired of drowning kittens or giving them away—I figure I'll raise one."

"I used to keep cats, but they always died on me," she said. "They'd get run over or the coyotes would eat them."

"Goddamn coyotes. They're a brought-in creature, you understand. They were never here until the interstate highway was built. Some connection there. Don't know's I can say what it is. But it's there, I'm sure of it."

He wants to stay, so charge him for the time, the Witch thought. But of course she wouldn't. She wanted to see what he was about. He reminded her a little of old man Williamson, except he was confident where Williamson had been resigned. That was because he was a rich farmer. Williamson never had a pot to piss in, nothing but that trailer on Black Swamp. Resignation had come by way of necessity. Hillary had land— family land. He had animals and machinery and buildings and prestige and know-how and friends who powered the world of Tuckerman County. Of course he'd be confident. What she liked about him was that his confidence was not the know-it-all kind (she thought of Aronson). Hillary wouldn't even think he was confident. He would merely live his life with confidence.

"You take tea or coffee?" she offered.

She made some coffee, the no-caffeine kind, and they sat at the kitchen table. He told her about his wife dying suddenly, and no kids home anymore. His last daughter was in the military. What kind of world was it when a high-school girl could join the Army upon graduation? Mostly, he talked about his dissatisfaction with the farm. He wasn't asking her advice, not even faking he was asking, as some men might. He just wanted to run off at the mouth as a man can to a woman but not to another man.

"That backhoe is mired deep," he said. "Thought for a while it was going to drop all the way to China. But this is New Hampshire—it sunk in three feet and hit ledge. During Melba's funeral all I could think about was how I was going to get the backhoe out of the mud. I pretty much reasoned it out too. I was going to drive a pole in the ground, anchor the tractor to it, and then hook up the tractor winch to the backhoe. The first thing I did after the burial was hustle out to the field, still in my suit and good shoes. I took one look at the backhoe, and it all came back to me. I said, 'Goddamnit,' and bawled my head off. Crazy."

"I'll take a hard hurt over a long hurt anytime," Estelle said.

Avalon looked at her appraisingly, the same look he had used to inspect the dried grasses. "You look different at your kitchen table," he said. "I'm not sure what to call you. Mrs. Jordan, or what?"

"Some men like to make believe I don't have a name. I'm Hey-You. But you know what most of the local fellows call me."

"Witch."

"Well?"

He frowned.

"My name is Estelle."

"Estelle—good. That's a fine name." He had something to call her by and that seemed to satisfy him as well as the sex had. In the same way, it satisfied her.

"I like that name Avalon. How'd you come by it?" she asked.

"My mother wanted to call me Harry. But the menfolk in the family named me after my grandfather's best bull."

91

Estelle giggled.

"It sounds like a joke, but it was serious business to my father and grandfather. Naming me Avalon was their way of thanking God for giving the Hillarys that bull."

"God?"

"God."

"I don't believe in God," she said. "I believe in stars and clockwork, and that's about it."

"I believed in God and then I didn't, and now I do again. Yes, ma'am. I'm convinced there's a Supreme Being. I don't know's he's a Christian or a Hindu or a buffalo, but I know he's out there."

"How do you know God's a he?"

"Manner of speaking—you sound like my daughter Julia."

"I ain't going to spit in your eye. How do you know he's a he?" There was sport in her tone, and that perked him up for the challenge.

"Well, it wouldn't be a she—that's obvious. So it has to be a he. Process of elimination."

They broke out into laughter.

"I didn't know you were going to be a kidder," she said.

"I didn't know either. I didn't know I was going to have fun, besides, you know—it."

"It," said Estelle, speaking the pronoun with the Witch's contempt. "We do it, we get sick by it, we die by it, we weep by it, we continue the race by it. We do it and we do it, and we never learn nothing from it. Good ole it."

Such talk usually put men off, scared them, but Hillary only looked at her half in amusement, half in amazement.

"What do you want to do?" she asked. "Go another round? Play some cards?"

"Go another round—how I wish I had the energy," he said, and laughed into his empty coffee cup.

She refilled it. "I do hope there is a God—he, she, or it, I

92

don't care," she said. "Just so's when I die, he, she, or it is eye-to-eye so I can give him a piece of my mind."

"He knows what he's doing." Avalon was serious now.

"If you were him, would you let go on what goes on and has been going on for thousands of years? You'd put an end to all this killing, this suffering, this stupidity." Estelle, too, was serious.

"You're saying that the average man or woman would do a better job as God than the one we got."

"Why, sure."

"You've got a feel for injustice, Estelle, but not for human nature," Avalon said. "You're not taking into account Original Sin or free will."

"Original Sin, free will—horseshit!"

"That's no argument."

"This is what happens when a man and a woman talk out a problem," Estelle said. "The woman calls a spade a spade, but she never gets her arguments down so's they line up one behind the other. Now a man can shoot half the people in New York City, and argue clean he done it for good reason—they were Reds, they ran drugs, whatever."

"That supports my original statement. God is a he." Avalon gave Estelle an I-gotcha smile.

"In that case, I'm happy to be on the downside," Estelle said.

That stopped him. He shook his head and smiled.

They talked on. When his cup was empty again, Estelle went into the living room and returned with the tie Avalon had left on the back of the chair. He took this gesture as it was meant, her signal for him to leave.

He stood, put on his coat, tucked the tie in the pocket of the coat, and made for the door. On the landing, he was suddenly awkward and formal. He was trying to find a way to thank her for the good time.

"It was all right," he said. "Not just 'it,' but the coffee."

"Instant and hot—that's how men like it," she said, ignoring his slight blush. "Why'd you put on a suit for it?" she asked.

"I own one suit. I put it on for weddings, funerals, and special occasions. Before I came here tonight, I brooded, wondering where to fit something like this in the scheme of things."

"You figured special occasion."

"Yah."

8

Critter in Upper Darby

Caddy-carried, Caddy-comforted, Critter Jordan and his wife Delphina sped into the hills of Upper Darby, headed for a party at the home of Roland and Sheila LaChance, Delphina's younger sister.

"No kids, no diapers, no dog—what a relief," Delphina said, squishing her big bottom into the plush seat of the Cadillac.

"Freedom—ain't it grand?" Critter said, although he wished she hadn't included Crowbar in her list.

He'd bought the five-year-old Cadillac from his Uncle Donald when finally he'd had a few extra collars in his pocket. The car served him on a couple of levels. It gave Delphina something to wheel around town in, and therefore got her off his back. More important, because it was a Cadillac it increased his ascendancy within the kinship. Never mind that he rarely drove it. The men in the clan understood that although Delphina might drive the car most of the time, it was Critter's car because only a man could possess a Cadillac since only a man knew what a Cadillac meant to a man. So went Jordan reasoning; Critter had no problems following it.

"We need to do something for ourselves once in a while," Delphina said.

Critter thought he heard a hint of forced contentment in her voice. He smiled to himself. He knew they'd be leaving the party around ten-thirty or so. Delphina would begin to miss her babies, find herself bored with adults, restless, and she would announce it was time to take her home.

Critter loved her, loved her dedication to their family. Family: that thing that had sprung up inside of, around, and between them that was not him or her or even themselves together, or even the two of them plus the kids, but something greater than the people involved.

"Family, once you're in it, you're in it—locked up," he whispered to himself.

"I wish you wouldn't mumble," Delphina said.

She was the core of the family. Without her, he and the boys would be nothing but drifters. He was proud of Delphina, proud of his children, proud of himself for making it as a family man. And yet marriage, family, business success, ascendancy within the clan, these great gains of his maturing years and the triumph and confidence they brought him were accompanied by a loss, like a grief, as if his dog had died. He saw no escape from this feeling. The farther he went in the direction he wished to go, the more distance he put between himself and something important he'd left behind.

"I'm happy but I'm not satisfied," he said.

"Are you going to be in one of your weird moods tonight?" Delphina said.

"I feel...I feel...I don't know. Alone," he said.

"You'll be all right—the people will be wall-to-wall at LaChances'." She talked to him the way she talked to their kids, and that made him want to hold her.

"I had a lousy upbringing," Critter said.

"Didn't we all," Delphina said, checking her face in the rearview mirror. He liked the way she smelled close up, like a bottle of perfume.

He'd been a lonely, confused boy, with a mother who had

abandoned him before he was old enough to know her and with a father who was self-centered and preoccupied with his own dramas in which his son was only a bit player. Critter had survived by thinking; mainly he thought about sex. But these days his mind was busied by practical thinking—fix, figure, buy, build, sell, swindle, borrow from Peter, pay Paul. There was much achievement but little fun in this. So he had mixed business and pleasure by opening the bookstore. It had stimulated him, but only for a while. He'd reached the point where he had to say a beaver is a beaver is a beaver. There must be more, he thought—"But what?"

"What do you mean, 'What?'" Delphina asked.

"Thinking out loud," Critter said.

"It's a wonder there was any noise at all," Delphina said.

My gosh, but she could be sarcastic.

They were off the blacktop now, the Caddy lazing over the dirt road that led into the Salmon Trust and the caretaker's house where the LaChances lived.

Delphina had gone along with the bookstore idea. She'd even work a shift or two to give Noreen some time off now and then. ("Anything for an excuse to get away from these kids," she said, but she didn't mean it.) He watched her finger through the raunchiest of the magazines and giggle. He told her not to take the plastic covers off them. It had troubled him that this good mother, this good wife, was herself so curious and forthright about sex. And it bothered him that in the bookstore Delphina could see what he saw; nothing of it was his own exclusively. The pleasure of his secret, sexual fantasy life was the secrecy as well as the fantasy. It loses something when you can't sneak it, he thought. A secret was to Critter's soul what a pizza was to his stomach.

The Caddy hit a bump, and Critter winced at the sound of the car's oil pan scraping gravel.

"You'd think they'd pave these roads," Critter said.

"'Course, you don't drive too fast," Delphina said.

Chance met them at the door. He was wearing blue jeans, ankle-top work shoes, a blue T-shirt and Soapy's old baseball cap. Critter reminded himself to call Soapy Sheila. Since she and Chance had got hooked up with the Upper Darby crowd, they'd become touchy about Sheila's old nickname.

He could hear Soapy playing the piano, and he watched Delphina slip away toward the sound of the music. Chance steered him toward a garbage can full of ice and beer. Chance took a Bass ale, Critter a Bud.

"Something you ought to know," Chance said, tugging unconsciously on his woodsman's beard.

Critter marveled at the transformation in him. Roland LaChance had come to Darby as a newspaper reporter, an outsider. But these days he talked like a native, dressed like a native, held forth on local issues. ("These out-of-staters come up here and they buy property and the first thing they do is post the land so's you can't hunt," he would complain. And what a joke that was, since hunting was not allowed on the trust lands of which he was the caretaker.) He had become more Darby than the homegrown stock.

"Shoot your wad," Critter said.

"There's a petition been started to shut down your bookstore," Chance said. "Mrs. Acheson is behind it. After they get a couple hundred people to sign, they're going to present the petition to the selectmen."

Critter eventually would take this news with the gravity it deserved, but for the moment it oddly buoyed him. A petition against him acknowledged he had become an important man in the affairs of Darby. He believed the real reason for the petition was people were jealous of him, and they didn't like someone from Darby Depot making a name for himself.

98

"Nothing they can do. I'm legal as trout in May," Critter said.

Chance seemed about to speak, thought better of it, turned, then struck up a conversation with a logger whose name Critter knew but had forgotten. They drifted away from him, until Critter found himself alone in the crowd.

He spotted one of the Butterworth girls filling a paper cup with wine. He sidled up to her, saying, "Tastes better when it's free, don't it?"

They chatted. He told her about the Caddy. She told him she was thinking about quitting college—funny name, Bad College. He told her he was a builder. She told him she had met a man who had built a birch-bark canoe. He fancied she fancied his looks. Some older woman called her name (was it Nestle?) and she slipped off through the crowd, and he waited for her to return, but an Upper Darby guy latched on to her, and Critter knew she'd be tied up for a while. He went after a beer.

He saw one of the Prell brats plant a wet kiss on the cheek of a woman with hair dyed pink. She laughed, cuffed the brat on the head; they parted. This, thought Critter, is what a party is all about: women, other men's women; cheap talk and cheap feels. He ached to express this thought, and he attached himself to a group of fellows talking about the pros and cons of the new mall in Tuckerman. Critter bided his time until there was a silence and he could interject his ideas about parties, but when the moment came he had forgotten what he was going to say. He was alone again.

He fetched a beer, slugging down half of it in a swallow. So the Acheson woman wanted to shut him down. Destroy his business. He imagined her blind drunk stumbling into the path of his oncoming Caddy. The violence of that thought, uncommon for him, suggested to Critter that the beer was taking hold.

"Feeling good," he said, but there was no one to attend to this remark.

Soapy stopped playing the piano, and someone cranked up the stereo and the party began to rock and roll.

Critter found the Butterworth girl and danced with her. But the song ended immediately after they started. She asked him to get her some wine. When he returned he couldn't find her. He drank her wine in a gulp, chasing it with his beer. He went in search of her again to explain the wonders of this new drink.

He bumped into Delphina. She was dancing with the logger. The next thing Critter knew Delphina was insisting he dance with her. So he did. It was kind of strange because the logger stayed on, the three of them dancing as if they were a couple. He and Delphina would make sweet love in the morning, provided, of course, he could wake before the baby did. They never made love directly after a party because he was always drunk and unfit for maritals, but later—*whooee!*

And he was alone again, the logger and Delphina somehow having danced to the other side of the room. He peeked at Delphina through the crowd, watching her swing her considerable ass around. It was as if she were someone else's wife.

Critter was on his sixth or maybe it was his eighth beer when he got sidetracked into the study. Here Chance and another man had set up a card table and they were playing chess. Critter recognized the second man as Hadly Blue, a professor at Tuckerman State College and the live-in lover of Persephone Salmon. Critter knew nothing about chess, but decided to watch for a while because Chance and Blue, in their concentration, hadn't noticed him, and he wondered how long he could stand not four feet away before they saw him.

"Check," Blue said.

Chance moved.

"Check," Blue said, moving a horse's head.

"Check yourself," Chance said, moving a tall piece with a crown.

Blue set his chin in his hands and went into a pout. "You put me in peril for my greediness," he said.

"That's chess, just like life," Chance said.

"Easier to beat you than life," Blue said.

Critter wished they'd hurry up and notice him, so he could leave. He wanted to dance.

Blue moved. "A little pressure for your queen," he said, smug now.

Chance immediately moved his tall piece the length of the board, and Critter could tell by the look in Blue's eye that his side was in trouble again.

"The queen transforms the pressure applied into her pleasure," Blue said.

"Yup." Chance was the cat that ate the canary.

"Why should the queen have so much power and king so little?" Blue said.

"Maybe chess was invented by an early feminist," Chance said.

"It is strange," Blue said, becoming animated. "Here's a game straight out of antiquity and yet the king is passive, an object of conquest, not the power but the lap of power, feminine, while the queen is active, a warrior—masculine. Kings behaving like queens, queens behaving like kings—something is amiss here, or perhaps a-Ms."

"Maybe king means kingdom—your move," Chance said.

"Maybe you guys ought to play checkers."

The gamesmen looked up at Critter. Like one four-eyed creature, he thought. Their education, the game, the queen-king stuff, the very world they came from, so different from the world of the kinship, united them. His personal tragedy struck him then. Outside the clan, he was lost.

"My father used to say I couldn't sneak up on the dead, but you can see how wrong he was—here I am," Critter said.

"Have a beer for yourself," Chance said.

Critter grinned—Ike's grin, a false thing; he could feel it contorting his face—and withdrew, not embarrassed exactly (he was too drunk to be embarrassed) but wary, an animal sensing a trap.

When he returned to the dance floor, he saw that Delphina was dancing with Garvin Prell, a lawyer and a member of the Upper Darby set. Critter was suddenly angry. He wanted to smash the man in the face, smash Delphina.

"I'm cutting in," he said.

"Cutting in." Prell groaned a laugh, and slipped into the crowd.

A slow song was on, and they waltzed, at times struggling to see who would steer whom which way, at times limp in one another's arms. Critter's anger passed, replaced by a feeling like fatigue; that is, he could say he was tired but he was also jittery. The people in the party seemed stupid and boring to him. They had nothing to say to him, he had nothing to say to them.

"Time to go home," he announced.

"It's only ten-thirty," Delphina said.

"I want to go home; I miss the babies," he said.

"You're drunk."

"I got something I want to tell you, something important. I want... I want... I want what I want."

"You've got the Cadillac," Delphina said, more puzzled than annoyed.

Delphina drove home. Critter rode in the back seat. He'd always wanted to ride in the back, like some rich guy being chauffeured. It amazed him what a smooth ride the Caddy gave. He imagined the Butterworth girl in the back seat with him. He wondered if she ever got her wine.

"Del?" he called.

"What?"

"Let's make like we weren't married and go parking."

"You really are drunk."

After she said that, he felt the distance between them widen. It was as if the Caddy were enormous, Delphina miles away. He sat there, not feeling bad exactly, but merely alone.

When they reached the blacktop, the Caddy made a whisper sound, like lovers cooing.

"Swing by the barn," he said.

"What in the world for?"

"I want to check on Noreen, make sure she isn't closing early on me," he said.

He didn't have to tell Del to wait in the car. She clutched the steering wheel impatiently. "Hurry up," she said.

"My sweetie." He meant to give her a little kiss, but as he spoke he was out of car, out of range.

"What?" she asked.

He didn't bother to answer, but weaved for the door to the bookstore.

Inside, he found Noreen, sitting on her stool behind the register, staring off into space.

"Hey-hey-hey," he called her, friendly like.

She almost fell off the stool with surprise, then giggled when she saw it was he who had startled her. By George, she was happy to see him.

"You may think I'm just a bad boss checking on his help at a late hour, but it's nothing like that." He was invigorated now. "It's just that the missus and I were—" He couldn't think of anything else to say.

"Oh, I don't mind you coming in. It gives me somebody to talk to," Noreen said.

"How's it been tonight—busy?"

"Earlier," Noreen said.

The red dress was a little loose on her. He wished it were tighter, but even so... "I thought I'd, ah, inspect the fire ex-

103

tinguisher. Town's down on us, looking for an excuse to lock our doors."

Believing Noreen was watching his every move, he took great pains to scrutinize the fire extinguisher. He put his hands behind his back. The fire extinguisher hung on a bracket on the wall. It was an old brass thing, left over from his father's reign of the auction barn, and he had no idea whether it would work.

"They can't get us on breaking no fire ordinance," he said.

"If they do, you'll figure something, Critter."

The sound of his name from her lips was like an embrace.

"Critter!" Delphina yelled from the Caddy.

On the remainder of the drive home, he savored the image of Noreen in her red dress, slightly off-balance as the sound of his voice reached her.

Noreen was an old story in the kinship, pregnant as a teenager, no husband, no education, her own parents divorced and disintegrated. She'd labored as an assembler in a factory, been laid off, collected welfare, clerked in a department store, been laid off, collected welfare, waitressed, left for personal reasons (feet), collected welfare, and so forth. She had lived with kin off and on, even though she much preferred having her own place. Even when she had work and cash, it was hard to find an apartment because landlords didn't like single women with children. Barely into her twenties, she'd gone through the hysterical stage, the anger stage, and the face-life stage, emerging a sort of zombie, stunned and impassive, as if someone had hit her between the eyes with a tire iron. She was kept from death and disintegration by the kinship, social service persons, her children, and luck. She was the perfect worker, beyond pain, beyond any idea of expectations. Critter knew all about this the way he knew the sky was blue on a sunny day, that is, unconsciously, without pity or sympathy, but also without contempt or condemnation, Noreen's plight part of the natural order of things. He'd hired her because he knew her type. He'd been right about her, too. Noreen did her job well.

He was proud of the way he had treated her. He hadn't laid a hand on her, hadn't made any indecent proposals, hadn't so much as copped a feel. He figured she must admire him for his restraint. Maybe not. People could be mighty ungrateful. Could be, too, she adored him. He mulled over this possibility. After what she had been through, Noreen would desire every man and no man. She'd give herself out of habit, probably even enjoy the actual nookie out of habit; then she'd wash her face and pop some bread in the toaster for the kids—habit. She'd be beyond desire, beyond love, beyond everything but habit. To give and not to get: that was what she was used to. He'd given her a job, hadn't smacked her or anything, hadn't made her do it with him, so she had good reason to be grateful— even to adore him. That was something to consider. A woman beyond love was not beyond adoration, in fact was subject to adoration. Religion proved that. If a woman adored you, she did what you asked without question. If a woman adored you, she was easy to satisfy, since your pleasure was her pleasure. If a woman adored you, she would do anything you asked and be a better person for the doing. There was only one way to discourage a woman who adored you and that was not to demand anything from her.

9

The Wig

The flea-market vendors were setting up their tables when Critter arrived with Selectman Crabb. The Witch didn't even have to look at Critter's agitated face to know something was wrong; the clipboard in the selectman's hand told her that. Paperwork was a weapon, sure as a gun.

They cruised the aisles in silence, Crabb stopping every now and then to write something down. After about fifteen minutes, they sat off in a corner at one of the tables. The Witch drifted over to eavesdrop. She knew men on men's business took no account of a woman.

"It's got the required number of fire extinguishers," Critter said.

"But it doesn't have a sprinkler system," Crabb said.

Arthur Crabb, like Avalon Hillary, was an aging valley farmer. In fact, he was Avalon's kin. The selectman's job was a hobby with him. He was known by townspeople to be pretty much on the up and up, as town officials went, and that made him easy or hard to deal with, depending.

"The bookstore has a sprinkler system, just like the ordinance says," Critter said. He was pleading with the old man, as a son will who knows he has no chance with his father.

"The ordinance states the system is required to cover the entire square footage open to public access."

"But the flea market's only open on Saturdays and Sundays," Critter said.

In the face of this irrelevant information, Crabb said nothing.

The silence seemed to incite Critter, alter the pitch of his anger from whining boy to injured man. "You people never enforced the ordinance before," he said.

"We had some complaints," Crabb said.

"I know the complainers—bunch of Upper Darby snobs." Critter stood, yanked by some invisible puppeteer. "My business is my business, and you can't shut me down as long as I meet the requirements of the ordinance."

"It's not the individual business but the parts of the building open to the public that have to meet the codes. Protect the public—that's the name of the game."

"You're telling me you can close my store just because these flea-market people don't have a sprinkler system?" Critter said.

Crabb rose slowly to his feet. He was fatigued but not intimidated by Critter's sort. "If there's a fire, it will burn the barn, not just the business that's offending the code," he said, paused, and added: "See the reasoning, do you?"

Critter moaned as if spat upon by a loved one. His mouth hardened up, his eyes widened, the worms inside them brightened. The Witch had seen that look before on a Jordan man; Critter was going to do something crazy.

He jumped on one of the tables and shouted, "Your attention please, your attention please." The urgency in his voice quieted the eighteen or twenty people in the barn. "Due to circumstances beyond our control, the flea market is hereby closed until further notice. Pack up your things and go home."

"But I paid for this space," Piper shouted.

"Yes, sir, you did," Critter shouted back, "and I'm going to give you a refund, not only for the week, but for the entire month. Come and stand in line now."

Puffed with self-importance and victory, Critter folded his

arms and faced the old selectman. "There—now you got no legal grounds to close my bookstore."

"Not today I don't," Crabb said.

After Critter had left and the vendors had finished their communal buzz (they whispered as if the barn were wired for sound), the Witch started bringing her things upstairs. She had stored her flea-market goods in the barn, and it felt strange to be moving them.

Why? The question, which she had no intention of addressing, seemed to form in the dusty air.

"You want some help lugging that stuff?" Piper asked.

"I can get it." She didn't want him to see the Witch's quarters.

He read something in her face, a fear, and he said, "This is not the end—there's other barns."

"Oh, sure," she said.

He left to load his pickup, then returned to say good-bye. He grasped her hand and shook it as if she were a man, an old buddy.

"Take it easy," he said.

She heard him on his way out, laughing sadly with the widow Kringle. Piper meant nothing to Estelle, and yet she couldn't bear to see him go. Piper, the other vendors, the flea market—these people, this thing, so outside her Witch self, brought her rest. Without them, there would be too much Witch in her. Like anything combustible, she risked being consumed in her own fire.

After she moved the last of her pots into the apartment, her rooms looked strange to her, not hers. She shoved things here and there, trying to regain a sense of familiarity, but everything she did seemed to make the place less her own. Finally she rose in fury, threw half the pots and weeds in the bedroom, and chucked the rest in the woodstove. The crackle of flames tripped in the tremor. She was okay now, righted by rage and desire.

She lit her pipe and went outside on her landing. The summer growth was so dense that she wouldn't have been able to see any sign of the Trans Am hidden in the woods, but anyway she sensed he wouldn't be out there. He followed her less and less these days, and when he did he kept a widened distance between them. He hadn't lost interest, she understood; he was biding his time, but for what purpose? The mystery frightened and excited her. What made her uncomfortable was waiting for him to act. She resolved to conjure on this problem, find a way to take the initiative in her dealings with the little monster. She stood, looking out over the hills for the longest time, but no ideas came to mind.

Later, restless, the toke high wearing off, she decided to drive to Tuckerman, buy some groceries.

Only a year ago, she might have stopped at Ancharsky's General Store in Center Darby Village, perhaps chatting with Joe, the proprietor, but lately she did all her shopping at the Magnus Mart in Tuckerman. She was never exactly comfortable there, and yet the place had an attraction for her. Maybe it was its immensity, not like a building, not like the outdoors, but like a world. You could rent a VCR movie, buy nylons, writing paper, or a prepared pizza as well as groceries. Maybe someday you could be born, grow, mate, give birth, and die in a Magnus Mart, without ever the bother of going outside. Unburdened by weather, sky, and earth, a body could curl up all peaceful, like a pear pyramided in a display, and just be.

She bought some apple sauce, a loaf of bread, margarine, fish on sale.

Her Subaru caught up to Noreen's VW just as the road dipped down on the straightaway in front of the barn. Moments later they were in the parking lot, walking to the bookstore.

"You follow close," Noreen said.

"I like it close," the Witch said.

Noreen was wearing her red work dress, but her hair wasn't combed, and her face was pale.

"Look at you, aren't you a disgrace," the Witch said.

Noreen blushed and her words poured out apologetically. "I'm late for everything, I can't help it—it's just the way I am—and so I have to rush rush rush in case Critter calls to check on me. I throw my dress on and put my makeup on soon's I open for business."

"Something for yourself on somebody's else's time—it's better that way," the Witch said.

Noreen fumbled with the key to the front door. Finally, the lock yielded and they went inside.

The place was unfinished, and likely would remain so, in keeping with Jordan fashion—just enough. Critter had nailed down wooden panels on the wavy barn floor, and that was that. There was no finish floor, no carpet, no linoleum. The gypsum-board walls were nailed up but left unspackled and unpainted. A few panels were missing in the false ceiling. Magazine racks were made of construction-grade lumber crudely whacked together and unfinished. The peep-show booths were raw plywood. In contrast to this background, the main counter consisted of a finely made oak and glass display case. The Witch recognized it as one of Ike's most favored pieces. He had spent almost a year of his spare time refinishing it. Now his son was using the case to show off dildos, penis rings, and inflatable dolls.

Noreen locked the front door behind her, then went into the back room to put on her makeup. The Witch followed. The room was crowded with stacks of magazines and boxes. The Witch saw a fire extinguisher on a wall, the door that led to the barn proper, a straw broom (rarely used from the looks of the place), a calendar (unmounted, showing the wrong month), a toilet, and a sink.

Noreen stood before the sink, over which was a doorless cabinet attached crookedly to the wall and holding a wicker bag, some Tampax, soap, and a toothbrush, its bristles badly mashed, ugly. Then the Witch saw a razor. The idea that Noreen kept something handy to cut with sent a shiver through her. She picked up the razor and removed the blade.

"What are you doing?" Noreen said, giggling with fright.

The Witch ran the blade lightly across her own wrist, not drawing blood but inscribing a pink-white line.

"You shave your legs with this?" the Witch said.

Noreen nodded.

"Relax, Noreen," the Witch said, and put the blade back in the razor.

"It scares me—it reminds me of my abortion." Noreen began to apply her makeup.

"You don't take any care, you just slop the stuff on," the Witch said.

"I don't like the bother. If I could afford it, I'd go to the beauty parlor every day and let somebody else make me beautiful."

"I knew a girl like you once—lazy, oh, so lazy." The Witch snatched a tin of powder from Noreen's hand. "I'll do your face. Start by washing it."

After Noreen was clean, the Witch led her, half-bullied, half-hypnotized, to the main room of the store. She sat Noreen on the stool in front of the register.

Fishing around for makeup in the wicker bag, the Witch found Noreen's birth-control pills.

"They screw up my period, but it's better than getting pregnant," Noreen said.

"I liked being pregnant," the Witch said.

"I can't remember if I liked it or not, I just was, and probably I didn't like it because I tend to forget things that give me grief," Noreen said.

The flesh of Noreen's face felt soft yet firm to the Witch's fingertips.

"I remember after the second one was born, I said, no more," Noreen said. "I took the pill, and then, well, it just sort of slipped my mind to take one every day. Wouldn't you know it, I was pregnant again. I cried and cried. My social worker says, 'Maybe you should consider an abortion.' One thing led to another."

"During my glory years, we had neither pill nor abortion doctors. You had the baby, or you learned to rid your body of it yourself. Today it's nothing. You go into the doctor's office, and there's a nurse and magazines to read while you wait."

"I didn't mind the operation—it was the hangover afterward that felt bad."

"I know," the Witch said.

Neither woman spoke for a minute, then Noreen said, "To be honest, I wanted my first baby, wanted it bad. After that, wanted to die."

"I also," the Witch said.

Noreen shut her eyes. The Witch could feel her relax under her fingers. In the hum of the neon lights she began to hear the drone of insects on a summer night from long ago, and the Witch in her dozed for a moment and her dear self spoke: "When I was a girl, my mother's love, her hands brushing my hair—and then one day she wronged me, not even sure how exactly."

"If you found out you'd feel better." Noreen talked as one repeating wisdom garnered from television.

"If I found out, I'd feel something I don't feel now. But better? I don't know," Estelle said.

After she finished putting makeup on Noreen's face, the

112

Witch stepped back to admire her work. It didn't look right.

"Lipstick's too pink, and we have to do something about that hair," the Witch said. "There's no shine to it, no body—it's scaggy."

"I didn't have a chance to wash it this morning."

"Or yesterday morning, or the morning before that."

"What difference does it make? Nobody notices."

"It makes every difference. A woman's hair is every bit of pride she has."

Noreen blinked with incomprehension.

It wasn't only that Noreen's hair was dirty, it was the wrong color, the Witch thought.

"You get on with your work. I'll be back," the Witch said.

She returned to her apartment and walked straight for the closet off the living room. She was excited, as if she'd learned someone had hidden a treasure among her own things. From deep in the back of the closet she pulled out an old hatbox. She blew off the dust and opened it. Inside was the wig she had placed there when her hair started to turn gray. She stood before the full-length mirror, holding the wig beside her. The wig was a little longer than her own hair, and the individual strands were straighter, darker, shinier. She put the wig on her head, and it was as if she had been injected with a drug that made her younger and more vigorous.

When the Witch entered the porn shop, pausing at the door, Noreen said, "What do you have in your hands, a black cat?"

Like an aborigine showing off a shrunken head, the Witch held out the wig with one hand.

Noreen giggled.

The Witch put the wig on Noreen's head. Then she wiped Noreen's mouth and held her own nighttime lipstick before Noreen.

"It's so red it's blue," Noreen said.

The Witch painted Noreen's lips, letting the color spill over

113

slightly to fill out the corners of Noreen's mouth. The Witch stepped back for an inspection. Satisfied, she removed Noreen's pocket mirror from the wicker bag and handed it to her. Noreen giggled at the image.

"I never liked my hair," Noreen addressed the mirror. "Another dirty blonde. So I dyed it real blond, like Hollywood. But it was such a hassle to keep. Always battling the roots. Gave it up. I never imagined black. I mean, like never. Now here it is—black. It's so... so different."

"It's getting late," the Witch said.

"Yah, time to open the store, go to work." Noreen returned the mirror to the bag.

"I'll make you up from time to time." The Witch patted Noreen's wigged head, and left the bookstore.

Outside in the parking lot of the barn, the Witch stared at the sun. The brightness hurt her eyes. She reached a hand upward, as if to touch the light. She felt like a drowning child reaching through the surface of the water for the rescuing hand of her mother.

While Noreen had been admiring herself in the mirror, the Witch had been staring at Noreen, as if Noreen herself had been the mirror, and the Witch had seen her own self from years ago. Now, under the hot sun, she was remembering another summer afternoon, the last hours of that girl, in a crowded shack, waiting for something, not sure exactly what.

Before Romaine spoke, Estelle recognized a change in her mother's eyes. They were far away.

"Your Uncle Oliver is visiting," Romaine said, not looking directly at her. "Wash all over. My brother likes folks to be washed."

She made Estelle clean up, change her clothes, put on a dress and shoes.

Then abruptly, Isaac, her father, took her on his lap, as he hadn't in years, it seemed. He told her a long rambling story that she did not understand, the way he used to before the booze took him over. They both laughed, Estelle because she felt the little girl in herself and was protected by that feeling.

Romaine brought Isaac a bottle, and he turned his attention to it.

She felt not anticipation at Oliver's impending arrival or apprehension at the change in her mother or anguish at her father's drinking, but oppressive closeness, the closeness of the shack, the closeness of the forest outside, like a sentence from a judge: confinement for life.

She watched from a window as a big car drove into the yard. It was like a ship from the sea; it promised her escape while it suggested dangers.

Oliver touched her hair almost absentmindedly so that she wasn't afraid. He said to Romaine, "I'll take her for a ride in my new car. These young ones like a nice, big car." His face was sharp, his body lean, and she liked the way he smelled, not boozy (she had it in her head that all men would smell of drink like Isaac and his brothers); he smelled of flowers (she hadn't yet learned about after-shave lotion).

"Have a drink?" Isaac thrust the bottle in front of Oliver. Oliver took a pull and gave the bottle back to Isaac.

"Go! Get away!" Romaine shrieked at Isaac, cuffing him with the flat of her hand. Isaac slunk off and lay on the couch. A moment later she could hear him snuffling. The sound caught her attention because she had never heard it before. It was when she realized the snuffling was a form of weeping that she also understood what was going to happen to her.

Romaine and Oliver crouched at the kitchen table, talking. She listened from the rocker by the window. She could make out some of their whisper-misted words.

"Not ready, not ready," Romaine said.

"I have eyes to see. She is ready."

"Her shape, yes."

"The spring has arrived in her," Oliver said. "See her skin, flushed—ready."

"Estelle!" her mother called from far away. Estelle rose from the rocker and rushed to her mother. Romaine kissed her cheek, brushed her hair away, and pushed her off.

"See how she clings to me. She clings. Even to him." Romaine pointed at the S of Isaac on the couch.

"She's spoilt, then," Oliver said.

"None of us been spoilt. We never had nothing. To be spoilt, you have to begin with something to spoil. We never had nothing," Romaine said.

"See how she waits, how she knows. Now I ask you, Romaine, I ask you."

She watched as Romaine moved farther and farther away. It was as if her mother's soul had departed from its body, embarking on a long journey into the stars.

"As you say—spoilt." Romaine's voice was flat.

"I will unspoil her," Oliver said.

Soon she didn't even try to listen, but immersed herself in the feeling, the incredible intensity of it, like hands on her body: the closeness.

Finally, Oliver turned to her and said, "I bet you never been in a new car."

She shook her head no.

"I bet you'd like to ride in a new car."

"Can I go for a ride?" She cried out, because Romaine was so far away.

"You see, she's eager," Oliver addressed Romaine.

"She is and she isn't. She's always been of two minds," Romaine said.

"Should I go?" she asked Romaine.

"It's a new car," Romaine said.

"Get in." Oliver took her arm.

She thought, Romaine is not here, Romaine is gone. She summoned her. "Romaine!"

"Go with him." Romaine's voice came from the great out there.

"Daddy!" she called.

Her father, who often lay passed out on the couch, now lay pretending to be passed out. She could tell by the sounds of his breathing, quick and shallow instead of slow and deep.

She liked the way the car rode, quiet and smooth.

Oliver didn't say where they were going. That made her feel as if she would never return to the shack, as if the big car was setting her free from shacks and boredom and anguish, taking her to something new and bright and tinkling, and on the other side of the world.

"Don't be a stranger now." Oliver reached over from the driver's side and pulled her close to him. At the urging of his hand, she lay her head on his shoulder.

"Isn't that better?" he said.

"I can't see too good."

"Okay." He released her.

She ooched up so she could see the road, but kept her head cocked at the same angle as when it leaned against his shoulder. Trees and telephone poles whizzed by. One, two, three... she lost count of the poles when she began to feel carsick. But soon she settled in, voluntarily close to Oliver, although not actually touching him.

"A car this big is a lot of push and shove to keep up," Oliver said. "Take you the morning to wash and wax her. Worth it, though. Protects the body. I like a shine you can see your face in."

She listened less to the words than to the voice, its sharpness, the way it sliced off words and held them out to her, like pieces of neatly cut meat.

"How far west you been, Estelle?"

North—she pictured the North Pole. South—she pictured a Florida orange. West—no picture came to mind; she couldn't think.

"Which way is that?" she asked.

He chuckled, enjoying her confusion. "Toward Vermont," he said.

"I been to Rutland," she said.

He laughed, a laugh that nicked her.

"I been to California, and I'll take you there someday," he said. "Once you've seen it, you'll never want to come back to Tuckerman County. It's big—grand. They got tree stumps big enough to put your momma's shack on. Once you've crossed the Golden Gate Bridge, you'll feel privileged forever."

She pictured the Golden Gate Bridge. The thought of it, the goldness her imagination endowed it with, made her believe Oliver would care for her, that he could do anything by truing it with his carving-knife voice.

As for the car, it was freedom itself—escape from shacks, from the messy New Hampshire forest pressing in, from the very smother of the kinship. The car would fly them to California.

He drove to the flood-control dam outside of Tuckerman. They watched the sun set over the water. He gave her wine to drink. Just enough. The wine was the color of the sunset, and it tasted like the sunset. He reached over and brushed against her, and she thought, Now it's going to happen, but all he did was roll down the window on her side so she could have a better view. The smell of him—male flowers—grew stronger. It wasn't until the colors of the sky merged and cre-

118

ated the night and a few stars were visible that he touched her.

And that was the end of the tenderness in him. He went at her like a dog.

It wasn't the loss of virginity that had been ruinous (she never valued it); it was the lies, the promises, the empty words, the betrayals—the car that, as it turned out, he didn't own, the fact that he had never been to California; but mainly it was Romaine, who for some reason had given her over to her brother. But why?

"Why?" the Witch whispered to the sky.

A week after the Witch made up Noreen, Critter paid a call to the bookstore around eleven P.M., closing time. The next night when the Witch heard his van pull into the drive, she decided to find out for herself what was going on. Already stoned, she restuffed her corncob pipe with toke and crammed it into one of the cups of her black lace bra. Like a battery, the still-warm pipe bowl against her breast charged her with energy. She crept down the stairs leading from her balcony into the maw of the barn. The only illumination was from the light that streamed through the half-open door of her apartment. The light distorted familiar objects, transformed them, it seemed, so their meaning lay not in their physical being but in their shadows; the shadows were feathers to the touch as she felt her way.

She bumped into one of the wooden posts that held up the barn. She put her arms around it, embracing it, exploring it, as she might the torso of a new lover. So much the hands knew. Hardness, softness, sharpness, bluntness, a thousand textures. The eyes taught the mind, but the hands taught the heart. The post was perhaps ten inches square, hand-hewn, its roughness filed by years. Time smoothed a thing, time

119

rounded a thing until finally the thing was something else.

When she found the door that led to the storage room of the porn shop, she allowed her hand to linger on the knob. It was cool, yielding, curvaceous; she would have sworn she felt the smell of metal in her palm. She turned the knob gently, and pushed until she felt the muted click of the bolt meet resistance. She slipped her nail file in the crack. The bolt gave way to the subtle pressure and the door opened. She stepped inside and quietly shut the door behind her.

She tripped into another world. The air of the barn had been light, cooling, restless; but the air in the back room was heavy, suffocating. The smells were young and simple—printer's ink, paper, piss. They made her realize how much older and more complex were the smells of the barn itself, consisting as they did of something of dust and sweat and varnish and mildew from the stuffing of chairs that retained the essence of the beer-swilling men who had lounged in them before thousands of television programs; and, too, the barn smelled after all these years of cow. She waited the longest time, hoping her eyes would get used to the dark. But they never did; the darkness was total, almost solid.

She groped about, touching smooth paper, rougher cardboard, feeling the grimy floor through the soles of her feet until she found the door that led into the bookstore. She opened it a crack. Light flew into her face like a hurled stone.

Critter and Noreen stood on the platform behind the store counter.

"Don't worry—nothing to worry over." Critter's voice was saturated with plan. He held Noreen in his arms; the Witch could see the backs of his hands on the shoulders of the red dress.

"I'm not worried—I'm afraid," Noreen said.

"Oh, shit, not that." He grinned as one before a child telling a tall story.

"Someone followed me again last night."

"What kind of car?" Critter humored her. He enjoyed her insecurity. It helped steam him up. Yet the Witch could see he wasn't the kind of man to hit a woman, and for that reason alone she believed it was Critter, not Noreen, who was vulnerable to a sudden reversal of the situation, he who might be struck down at any moment.

"A shiny car—black, I think."

"You've got to do better than that, Noreen. What make car— Ford, Chevy, what? You get the plate number? Was it the same car as before?"

"I don't know—I'm just scared."

Critter stroked her neck. Noreen baits her trap with her own fear, the Witch thought.

"You're tired and jittery when you leave, so you imagine every car that gets on your tail is following you," Critter said.

"No, I'm being followed."

"Okay, you're being followed." Critter's hands fell from Noreen's shoulders to her waist, then to the tops of her buttocks.

"Critter, you keep right behind me when I leave. Promise."

"Sure." He was concentrating on his pleasure.

"Every night. Promise."

Critter stopped fondling Noreen. "Not every night," he said. "I have a home life, I have things to do."

"Promise—please."

"It's nothing. It's the late hour. It'll be all right." Critter tried to sound reassuring, kindly, but failed. His own father Ike, the Witch's son, never had the gift for kindness. Critter had it, but had not the means for expressing it.

Noreen trembled, and her fear rippled outward, to Critter, to the Witch. So the Trans Am was following Noreen. He'd get her, too, like he'd never get the Witch, she thought. The Witch trembled, half with Noreen's fear, half with her own desire.

"Tell you what," Critter said. "I'll put a CB in your VW. You get in any kind of trouble, call the Van Man."

"A CB." Noreen cooed; it was a proclamation of victory. "I'll need a handle."

"Red Dress," Critter said, and as if by magic, the dress fell from Noreen's shoulders. She stood in panties and bra, no stockings; the black wig, long and flowing, made her face look small. Critter leaned into her, kissing her throat, reaching around behind and unhooking her bra. Noreen cooed again.

She sounds like some disgusting pigeon, the Witch thought. She was jealous of the quality of that coo. It came natural, you couldn't fake it. Worth money it was.

Critter stepped back and said something. The Witch heard only the word *model*.

Noreen slipped off her underpants.

Critter left the Witch's view for a moment, returning naked except for his shoes and socks, and a camera dangling from a strap around his neck. Noreen struck a pose. Critter took a couple of pictures, the afterbursts of the flash lingering menacingly in the Witch's mind. Critter pressed himself against Noreen, pressed her against the counter. In their passion, they appeared to be fighting. Critter withdrew; he couldn't make up his mind whether to take pictures or make love. In the end, he did both poorly. Noreen behaved as one learning to swim, all awkward and frenzied.

Afterward, Noreen put on her dress, sat upon her stool, and she and Critter drank bottles of beer in silence, not even looking at one another. Critter downed his beer and began making advances at Noreen again.

"I'm not finished," she said.

"The beer can wait—I can't." Critter began to pull the dress over Noreen's head.

"You'll rip it," Noreen said.

"I paid for it, I can dang well do with it what I please."

"But you gave it to me. You said it was mine."

Critter released Noreen and threw up his hands. "I get that stuff at home. I don't need it in my place of business."

"Promise to buy me a new dress if you rip this one." Noreen bowed her head, as one surrendering herself.

Oh, what a cunning one you are, thought the Witch.

"I'll buy you a new one anyway." Critter yanked the dress over Noreen's head. It did not rip.

Noreen cooed. Critter took some more pictures and did it to her again. Better this time. The Witch wondered why they hadn't gotten a mattress to put on the floor. Perhaps the difficulty and discomfort of the position—in part standing, in part seated, but never reclining—made the act seem not like sex but some combination of fantasy and penance, misconduct pardoning itself.

When they finished they rushed to get their clothes on; they resembled comedians in a silent movie. On their way out, Noreen said, "You're going to follow me home now."

"Most of the way."

"And the CB—when do I get that?"

"I'll install it first thing next week."

"And my new dress?"

"What?"

"You promised."

When they'd left and the Witch was alone, the scene with Critter and Noreen began to twist about in her mind. There was a moment when she wasn't certain who had been out there. Herself? Was the man a stranger? Then the images came clear again, and she could see them—a man and a woman, struggling.

10

Supercow

"What goodies do we have here?" Avalon Hillary reached into a brown paper bag Estelle had brought.

"Home cooking," Estelle said.

"Oh, sure. That's why it says Magnus Mart on the plastic wrap."

"I'll take it back and you can eat one of your cows."

"The sandwich will do, the sandwich will do." Avalon bit into the Italian grinder, rolling his eyes in imitation ecstasy.

They were sitting at Avalon's kitchen table, the weary old farmer and the weary old whore. He was almost never in the house, but he had installed an answering machine on his telephone, and when Estelle wanted to visit she'd leave a message: "Something to satisfy your appetite 'round six o'clock." She always bought the same thing—a grinder, an apple, a pint of cranberry juice. He never complained, and he never offered to pay her back; she liked that. They'd talk for an hour or half the night, depending on whether she had a customer later.

"Wonderful grinder. And an apple fit for a king," Avalon said, the usual mock "whoopee-doo" in his tone.

He took a large bite out of the grinder, holding the apple in the other hand, as if for balance. Then he put the grinder down and chomped into the apple.

"You've mighty good teeth for an old poop," Estelle said.

"Must be the milk my mother made me drink." He held up the apple, the bite out of it glistening with moisture that rippled Estelle with a small fright. "If I had to do it over again, I never would have involved myself in the family dairy business. I would have sold the herd the day my father died and planted some of those Granny Smith apple trees. Be a millionaire today and there'd be no cowshit under my shoes."

Estelle popped the top from the juice bottle, tore a paper towel from the rack over the sink, and tucked it into the throat of his shirt. He smelled of the outdoors. Avalon worked all day, worked alone, so when she arrived it was natural he would want to ramble. Estelle was content to listen.

"Today I eat at all hours, when I goddamn please, thank you." He took another bite of the grinder, following it with a swallow of juice. "But I used to eat three meals a day, big meals, too, at six o'clock, twelve o'clock, and again at six o'clock at night. At five of the hour I'd drool for my feed. Six, twelve, six—magic numbers for the stomach, a way of life. If I missed a meal, I'd be grouchy for a week."

"You fool," Estelle said, joking, one friend to another.

He shook the juice bottle at her and, pretending to be cross, said, "Why do you buy this stuff? It goes right through me."

"At your age, things go through too fast or linger too long," Estelle said.

Avalon chuckled. "Actually, I think I'm better off this way, going skimpy on the food. Better for health—I think. I don't know. Truth is, after all these years of trying to figure, I figure I don't know a goddamn thing. It was Melba had the where-withal in this household, pure instinctive knowledge of life."

Estelle turned her eyes away, signaling she didn't like him mentioning the name of his late wife. She didn't mind his frequent reminiscences regarding her green thumb or her housekeeping skills or her all-superior way of handling door-to-door salesmen, as long as he kept a distance between his living self and the deceased one, referring to her as "she" or "the wife." But when he used her name—Melba—Estelle could feel herself grow sick with dull anger and loneliness. The fact was she wasn't used to her affection for Avalon. Didn't have a word for it. *Like* and *respect* weren't strong enough; *love*—no it couldn't be love; it must be some kind of feeling she couldn't identify because it was new to her, because a man like Avalon was new to her. He was no Williamson needing an escort to the grave, no Oliver abducting a partner for hell, no Aronson hiring a whore for his dreams. He was a man, a real, bona fide man.

Later, after he'd eaten and drunk most of the decaf coffee she'd made, a worried look came across his face. She thought she knew what troubled him. They'd been seen together. People were talking. Farmer Hillary was keeping company with the Jordan Witch. She wondered whether he worried more that she tainted his good name or the memory of his dear wife.

"You look tired," she said.

"Tired of this farm."

So, she'd been wrong. He wasn't worried about his whore; he was worried about his property. Important things first.

"Well?" she said, knowing he'd want to talk.

"No doubt about it, I'm through with farming," he said. "This place is full of ghosts. I mount my tractor and I see my father falling from it, dislocating his shoulder; I turn a clod of earth and I feel the hand of my grandfather on the ash shovel grip he carved. I watch the sun set over the trees in the west, and I see my children staring daggers at me because they hated the work and worry of this place. Yet the land holds me. Mainly, I like the grass, like to cut it, smell it, watch it in the sunshine. It's the farm I need to get rid of, the goddamn cows. I got this nutty idea when the cows go the ghosts will pasture out."

"So?"

126

"So, I'm going to hold a cow auction, Estelle. Besides the land, the cows are the only thing of value here. House is tired, barn swaybacked, tools worn. But these cows, especially my Bess—top girl in this county—have some oomph in the marketplace."

"You got one special cow?" Estelle was suddenly suspicious.

"Bess is my supercow, worth more than all my milkers put together, plus you, and me, and a congressman. Sometimes I think I'm prouder of Bess than of my own children."

"Grateful for what you've done for her, is she?"

"Now don't be smart with me." He spoke with loving condescension. "I'll say this: I bred her into being and I raised her right. And she lives pretty good today, gets the best of feed and medical care and never worries about heaven, hell, or oblivion. Goddamned but if in her own way she isn't grateful. Unlike my children, she doesn't give me any back talk and she pays her way, and I can sell her, which you can't do with your kids and still save your soul."

"I don't see how you can call a cow 'super'; she's only meat on the hoof." There was something wrong, but Estelle wasn't sure what it was. Perhaps it was Avalon's attitude, a certain twist in logic. Bess was his supreme accomplishment. Now he had to cast her off, sell her because the price she fetched would measure the accomplishment. She thought of Oliver and how he would be angry and hurt if a customer wouldn't meet his price for her.

Avalon smiled wryly. "I believe you're jealous."

"Not jealous—amazed. Amazed a member of the male kind shows such a high regard for a member of the female kind. It's just that—"

"—that you don't get it."

"You're teasing me again."

"I suppose I am." He showed his fine teeth. My, he was

smug. He knew she knew he had a little secret and that she wanted to know it. As men will with a woman, he toyed with her by withholding the knowledge.

But, the Witch's cunning rising in her, Estelle folded her arms over her breasts and waited close-mouthed for him to make the next move. The gesture and the tactic of silence caught him off-guard. She'd remembered him saying his wife used to cross her arms and clam up.

"You come by Tuesday, around nine o'clock in the morning," he said. "Serviceman will be here, and we'll show you what makes Bess a supercow."

"Suppose I don't care," Estelle said.

"Come by anyway and keep an old farmer company." Avalon's voice turned suddenly gentle, the smart-aleckiness gone from it.

He took her to his bed then and slowly and by degrees she roused him and made love to him. No money exchanged hands. Love itself was the payment.

He let his contentment run its course before he allowed that worried look to return to his face. She understood. Like any practical-minded man, he shelved a worry during a meal, during love-making, during the gloom of another worry.

"Okay, what is it?" she said.

He began to speak, caught himself, and prepared to start anew. She guessed he was going to say she could read his mind like Melba used to, but she was wrong, had been wrong from the start about what had been troubling him.

"Estelle, I got a pretty good idea who almost ran you down that day in my field," he said.

Stay away, stay away—she thought for a moment she had uttered these words, but apparently she must have just looked at him quizzically, because he talked on as if answering a question.

"I wasn't going to mention it because I was afraid it would

upset you," he said, "but it's best you know, and maybe be a little upset, so's you keep your guard up. I've been on the lookout for that black car around town ever since that day. I've seen it four or five times. Knew I would. To find a fella does his thinking and mischief in his car, keep your eye on the road. I recognized the driver, Upper Darby stock. They've got six or eight or maybe twenty black sheep up there on the hill where the Salmons, the Prells, and the Butterworths live—they specialize in black sheep—and this fellow's one of them, pure pewter black sheep."

The Witch didn't want to listen. She didn't want to hear that the Trans Am was human, belonging to time and place. She wanted him on the road and in her mind, just as she wanted Noreen Cook before her like a mirror of the past, the two of them ripples of her tremor.

"When I spotted him I garnered as much on my own," Avalon continued. "Then I talked to Mrs. McCurtin, who was only too happy to fill me in on the details. Kid's name is Dan or Don or Dane, something like that. His mother is Natalie Acheson. Runs the boutique in the barn over there at the old Swett place?"

The Witch nodded, imitating Estelle's intentness for Avalon's words.

Avalon was fooled and went on with his tale. "Seems as if Mrs. Acheson used to be married to one of the Butterworths and they had this one boy. The marriage soured, the father left to live in San Francisco or some other such place at the other edge of the continent, and the mother remarried the Acheson man. The boy lived here, lived there, spent a lot of himself in private schools. Nobody really wanted him, I suppose. Eventually, he ran off, lived on the streets, or so the story goes. Of recent, he got into some kind of trouble, bad trouble. Mrs. McCurtin says probably drugs, but I could tell she was just speculating. Anyway—bad trouble. He's on probation, that much is known. Sounds to me, Estelle, like this is a nasty young man. I advise you to keep your distance from that car, and if he gives you even a horn honk, call Constable Perkins."

"You say the car you saw was black," the Witch said.

"Black as one of my holsteins is black and white."

"The car that almost ran me over was blue."

"No, Estelle, it was black."

The Witch shook her head gravely. "Blue," she said.

"Blue, you say. Why I must be getting old not to know black from blue." Avalon grinned, glint of steel in his eye. He was beginning to see the Witch.

In her Witch's knowledge, Estelle Jordan knew the car was black, knew her lie and its purpose, to protect the Trans Am. She reveled in the lie. In the sadness of the lie resided the dear self.

"In a bruise, sometimes you can't tell black from blue," she said.

"Do you think my face is okay?" Noreen said, looking up with cow eyes, as the Witch rubbed dark purple mascara with her little finger in a crescent under one of those eyes.

"Your face is your own until I touch it, and then it's mine." The Witch's answer was sharp. The question had disturbed her, not because she couldn't deal with it, but because it suggested to her that Noreen was a person, with opinions, feelings, thoughts, questions. Noreen was not a person, Noreen was not even real, Noreen was a reflection.

"You scare me but I like it—you're like a movie," Noreen said. "Is that why they call you 'Witch'—because you scare people?"

Estelle remembered the day her son Ollie had named her Witch. The sky was flat but restless, like the surface of a pond. She could see rows of stones. She didn't believe that farmers had made those rock walls; Indians did for religious reasons

130

long forgotten. Blood seeped from the stones. And then her mind was back in the present. The storeroom of the porn shop, where nearly every day she made up Noreen's face, was dreary, disheartening in its ugliness. How ugliness wore away at the soul.

"It's a long story. It makes me sad to tell it." The Witch let her hands linger over Noreen's face, as if its beauty in her fingertips could decorate the room.

"But you wouldn't be anything else but what you are—the Witch: famous?" Noreen sought reassurance.

Estelle laughed darkly and privately, like a child hearing confirmation that wolves lurked in closets of her house.

Noreen looked up. "I know you don't really like me," she said. "Why do you make me up? Why do you do this for me, Estelle?"

Noreen's use of her name, sudden and unexpected, pierced the Witch like a musical note.

"I don't do it for you, I do it for me," she said. "Why do you put up with the abuse I heap upon you?"

"I don't know." Noreen waited for an answer to the question the Witch had posed to her. The Witch's answer would be *the* answer.

"You like my hands on you. Admit you like my hands," the Witch said.

"I like to be pampered. Nothing wrong with that," Noreen said, growing content under the Witch's familiar scorn.

"Shut your eyes now, relax, get some rest before you go to work."

Noreen looked into the Witch's eyes, seeing bright little eels in them. Soon she shut her own eyes, and fell pleasantly into a half-doze.

"How do you feel?" Estelle asked.

"I don't know—like, like I'm cozy, hiding."

"Like a lamb—you feel like a lamb."

131

"Yes, I feel like a lamb." Noreen drifted off.

She has no real being, the Witch thought. She becomes whatever people say, whatever they want. All she gets out of it are things. But there is no she; there is no Noreen.

After Noreen and Critter had closed the porn shop, the Witch stole into the storeroom, made her way to the main showroom and snapped on the overhead lights.

Her eyes were drawn to the magazine racks. So much color on shiny paper glistening like hardened sweat, all in service of making private parts public, every sex act she'd ever heard of and then some, women with men, women with women, men with men, women and men alone, women with objects, women with animals, twosomes, threesomes, foursomes, and -somes so many the organs got in each other's way, all the races integrated, pretty people and homely people, even a magazine devoted to fat ladies. She figured they'd have to pay the models double, once for the picture-taking, once for the sex. I bet these girls make a good living, she thought. An image flashed in her mind of a used-car lot, pennants slapping in the breeze, old boozer standing around with a cigar in his mouth— she was too old. Double pay, immortalized on film—not for her; she'd missed out. When she was young, she'd had a terrific body and nobody had actually appreciated it. She herself hadn't even realized the glory of it until it was past its prime. Men had looked her over and taken the goodies, but they'd never taken the time to appreciate what was there, never perused at their leisure, as today they might peruse one of these magazines. Another image: ruins of a temple shown in the *National Geographic* magazine. Of course she was as good as ever in her trade, maybe better because of the gum-it skill. But you couldn't show a toothless old woman in pictures and put the idea over. She looked again at the magazines in their racks, now seeing Noreens everywhere. Hundreds of Noreens, firmly

boobed, long-legged, toothed, eager, dumb—oh, so dumb—
or so smart they could fake oh-so-dumb.

Running off the main room was a short, dimly lit corridor
with peep-show booths on each side. She opened the door to
a booth. It was no more than five feet long, three feet wide;
there was a bench against the back wall and a white panel on
the inside face of the door. Apparently you sat on the bench
and looked at the panel where dirty movies were shown, and
upon which men had written crudely of their yearnings. Her
eye took in pictures of penises and vaginas, telephone numbers, lines of verse, messages. Perhaps some men came here
not to view the peep shows but to sit upon the benches and
contemplate what was writ, then to offer their own words. Was
this what men scared of flesh did in place of touch—write of
their desires? Some of the messages pleaded, some joked, some
screamed in anger. So many men had their peckers hooked
netherwise to their feelings of rage; anger and sex were different strokes of the same piston.

Something like a parking meter hung on a wall inside the
booth. This, she realized, was the thing you put the tokens in
to play the movie. The Witch rummaged around behind the
counter, looking for tokens. The cash drawer was on the floor,
shoved under the counter, the big bills gone. She found a
console box for a burglar alarm, wires sticking out of it. Critter
had had the foresight to bug the place but not the fortitude to
follow through with the work.

She spotted a cardboard shoe box on a shelf in the cabinet;
inside was a stack of nude photographs of Noreen. She seemed
frailer in the pictures than in the flesh, thighs scrawny, breasts
pubescent, smiling shyly, her face too small for the black wig
that covered her natural hair. In love with the camera, a girl's
harmless crush. The tremor thumped like a beating heart inside the Witch.

Hanging on a peg behind the counter were some keys. The

Witch returned to the booth she'd been in before; eventually, she felt the yielding of lock to key tremble through her fingertips. Tokens spilled out. She put one in the slot and settled in on the bench.

The movie began with no credits, no titles. Four men and a woman sat around a card table in a room furnished cheap and new; a motel room, as later the Witch figured out. The men were pool-hall wise, pool-hall sexy, the woman all too familiar—young flesh, old spirit, soft body, hard face, thick hair, thin hands. The movie was in color, no sound but the *hiss-click* of the projector. This suited the Witch. She didn't care to listen to a bunch of grunts and groans. The sounds of sex had always struck her as flotsam to the act itself. She was reassured by the noise of the film projector. It suggested that no matter what people did, no matter their pleasure or pain, the machinery of the universe ground on unawares, uncaring, but also uncritical.

The woman won all the chips on the table, laughed and left. Good for her. The screen went dark. The Witch put another token in. The men discovered they had been gypped, although how was not made clear. That troubled the Witch. Perhaps the woman hadn't cheated the men after all. Perhaps she didn't deserve whatever was going to happen to her. It was like watching a tragedy develop on television. She was both entertained and horrified; she had to know the end. The men abducted the girl. A gang bang followed. Rough stuff. Sucky-fucky. Cornholing. But no ending. The men shot their wads and the movie stopped, the fate of the card cheat unknown. The cost had been eight tokens.

The Witch shut her eyes and she could see and feel a shower of color from the movie rain down upon her.... Did they kill you? Or only scorn you with sex? Maybe you escaped. Maybe you killed them. The uncertainty, the fact that the uncertainty would never be resolved, made the Witch think about Romaine. Why did you surrender me to Oliver that day? Was it only because I was a nuisance or a burden?

She drifted around the porn shop like one on a rudderless ship, playing the peep shows, reel after reel, over and over again, so that eventually time and memory lost their meaning for her. She immersed herself in the sex acts of the movies; she became part of them. Perhaps she was not here, but in there, in the movie, and this old whore's body was make-believe. It didn't matter. There was no fear in her, no anger. She dived through time: *You'll never make it without my help, Noreen. Critter might lead you home tonight or tomorrow night and the night after that. But there will come a night when you'll be alone, and he'll be there, in the woods, parked, ready. He'll have you and he'll kill you, and I'll have you and I'll kill you.*

She returned to the booth with the movie of the woman at the card table. She put a token in, another, another. And she was seeing kin dancing to fiddle music on the wooden floor of a town hall. Which town? She reached out for a hand, reaching for her mother in a crowd, and the image vanished and she was looking at the porn movie. For the dozenth time the men caught the girl who had deceived them; for the dozenth time the mystery of the girl's fate scourged the Witch.

Exhausted, back in her apartment, the Witch washed and scrubbed the makeup from her face. She brushed her hair, dressed in a flannel nightgown, retired to the little bed in the far room, and lay down to sleep. A few images from the porn shop lingered in her mind, but they were like far-distant memories, vivid but removed from this dear self.

The sky was overcast the day Estelle headed for Avalon's barn and an encounter with his supercow. It felt like rain. In the auction barn's parking lot, Estelle watched the giant snapping turtle in some grass. Its head fully extended, neck stretched out, the turtle seemed to be reaching for the warmth of a sun determined to remain hidden, the crooked edges of its mouth like a cruel grin.

"What do you want?" Estelle called, as if to a wandering boy. The turtle did not respond.

When Estelle reached the Hillary Farm, the sky was even darker, lower, then when she'd left.

Avalon wore his usual work gear—blue denim overalls, blue cotton shirt, John Deere cap, and the black rubber boots he called shitkickers. And yet he had a gleam in his eye, like a man dressed up and slickered down for stepping out on the town.

They strolled into the barn together. Instantly, the barn air chilled her. The interior was cold, raw, dark, a triumph of gloom over the outside weather itself. In the auction barn, the smell of the past was weak, corrupted. Here it was strong, pure, no different today from a century ago. Nothing was new; metal was pitted or rusted, wood weathered and cracked. Even the spiderwebs seemed ancient. Like Avalon with his sloping shoulders, wide hips, and jowly jaws, the barn appeared to sag, from the weight of its own presence over time.

"This place makes me feel uncomfortable, unwelcome," she said.

"It's because you're not a cow," Avalon said.

She confronted him. "You invited me here to watch you breed your Bess, didn't you?"

"In a manner of speaking."

"I know the act. It's not much different among animals than people, and I've had experience."

"This one time, Estelle, you are wrong—far, far wrong. Among farm animals the act is nowhere like natural. What

136

you're going to see this morning is science having knowledge of nature at her most serious moment. I'm speaking biblically now." There was no hint of the usual humor in his voice.

They descended into the guts of the building. This, she thought, is a place that has never seen strong light. Furthermore, she guessed her skirt at this moment had brought in more color than anything else over the history of the barn.

"There's my Bess." Avalon pointed to a cow tightly confined in a stall.

Something about the way he said "Bess" disturbed Estelle. It was the "my." The "my" took away from the identity of the cow. It occurred to her then that Bess was no name at all. A wise man wouldn't recognize a personality in a creature he planned to kill or use for commercial gain. The name Bess must have been a joke, mere man's play. Every cow was Bess. Estelle felt a slap of humiliation on behalf of Bess.

Someone hollered, but the air of the barn distorted the shout so the words were garbled. A shiver of danger ran along Estelle's spine.

Avalon recognized her fright. "Nothing to be worried about, old girl. Only the serviceman, nervous because I wasn't at the door to meet him. Wait here." He ambled off.

Alone, Estelle studied Bess. In the restricted area of her stall, she seemed immense, both burdened and exalted by her own bulk. She munched absentmindedly on some hay, neither contented nor concerned, but resigned, reminding Estelle of scores of Jordan kin, especially women, souls who had struggled to figure out this much: that they were incapable of understanding what their lives were all about.

Avalon returned in a few minutes with the serviceman. He was a thin fellow with a shoe-box face and a black mustache the size and shape of a bow tie. He was dressed in white coveralls, stained along the thighs with some kind of yellowish stuff that wouldn't come out in a wash. He never looked at Estelle, nor did Avalon introduce them. She was not part of the business at hand, and therefore she did not exist. Estelle stepped back and brought her hands to her face, to feel the reality of her physical being.

Avalon threw a rope around the cow's neck and jerked her hard, to get her started out of the barn. He led her down a long corridor, Estelle and the serviceman following. The wooden floor of the barn shuddered under Bess's footfalls. Estelle caught the serviceman sneaking a looksee at her. This made her feel as if she'd won something from him.

Although the day was cloudy and dark, the light outside, by comparison with the barn's, seemed brilliant, a gray glare. The serviceman threw up a hand before his eyes. Bess blinked, then bellowed. Estelle resisted the urge to run back into the barn. Only Avalon had anticipated the change in light, and he greeted it with a smile.

Avalon tied Bess to a stake driven into the ground, and the two men circled her, sizing her up. Estelle stayed back, standing in tallish grass; she could feel a moist coolness on her bare legs.

The serviceman said something she didn't catch. He talked fast with an accent she wasn't familiar with. She gathered he wanted to get the job over with, had more important things to do. Avalon taunted him by taking his time.

"She won't complain," Avalon said. He took Bess's huge face in his hands, looked into her brown, watery eyes like a hypnotist, then released her and whacked her on the neck with a blow that would have felled a man. Estelle understood this passed as a pat to a cow, but the roughness disturbed her. Men were always looking for an excuse to whack something, even in displays of affection.

"She wasn't too steady last time—tried to kick me." The serviceman fiddled with his equipment, a wood-grain metal unit with dials on it from which protruded a coiled hose; its silvery nozzle seemed poised to strike.

"You rushed her, my boy," Avalon taunted. "You can't rush these old girls, and you have to show 'em a kind hand."

"You always say that, Mr. Hillary," the serviceman said.

"My girls." Avalon spoke ironically.

The serviceman chuckled nervously, then shut down signs of emotion on his face. He put on eyeglasses and pulled clear plastic gloves over his hands, holding them up to the weather, like a doctor before an operation. He appeared very intellectual now, very impressive. Estelle sensed a change in the situation. The serviceman was no longer under Avalon's thumb; the serviceman had become the boss.

"Hold her steady," he commanded. The hose seemed to uncoil of its own will, the nozzle taking a position in the plastic-gloved hand of the serviceman.

"Hang on, Bess, we're going to delve into your future," Avalon said. He half draped himself over Bess's neck.

Nozzle and hand disappeared inside of Bess. The serviceman rummaged about in Bess's uterus, at one point shouting to Avalon, "Hold her! Hold her!"

Bess heaved and sighed, and stomped a foot heavily as if to the beat of music. The hose slipped out for a second.

"Bastard!" the serviceman grumbled.

"Steady, steady as she goes. Going to be okay, girl." Avalon reassured Bess, but to Estelle's ear there was a coldness about him, or perhaps a remoteness, at any rate a lack of recognition of Bess as something alive, as being anything more than a tractor or that cadaver of a backhoe in his field. Estelle wanted to shout, "Can't you treat her like she's human?" But of course that was stupid. So she stood there, stunned and helpless, not knowing why she felt like a witness to a crime.

Intense but cautious, the serviceman busied himself inside Bess. He was, thought Estelle, like a small boy poking a hole in the ground with a stick, imagining that inside is a snake. When he was done, he had sucked out the deepest, richest ore of Bess's femaleness.

Avalon grabbed some plastic gloves, slipped them on, dipped his hands into the creamy mucus, and held it before Estelle. His face was flushed with pride or victory or ecstasy, something, some man-thing she could not fathom.

"There, look," he said in bragging tones. "Isn't it a miracle? Eight, ten, maybe twelve fertilized eggs. Too small to see, but there. A miracle of being and science. Understand now why this Bess is a supercow? What we have here is a daughter of science, business, and God. You understand, Estelle?" The heat of his emotion radiated outward.

"Those eggs won't grow right outside their mother's belly," Estelle said.

"She doesn't quite get it." Avalon addressed the serviceman.

Calm, detached, the serviceman explained, "For years we extracted semen from the best bulls and bred cows with it. But the best milkers drop only so many calves. Suppose we bred only the best milk-producing cows with the best bulls? Now we can do that. We take a cow like Mr. Hillary's here and we give her drugs to divide her eggs and bring her into heat. Then we artificially inseminate her with the sperm of a prize bull. What we did today was flush the fertilized eggs from her uterus. They'll be surgically implanted in the wombs of lesser cows. This grand milk-producer here will never have to carry to term."

"We can make this Bess breed five, ten, twenty, fifty, a hundred or more of her own kind," Avalon said. "You see now why we call her a supercow?"

Estelle looked at Bess. The cow was munching grass, oblivious to what had just happened to her. Estelle looked at the sky. It was starting to clear up. Calves would be born. Sons and daughters, mothers and fathers—far away from one another, motherhood immaterial.

11

Romaine

Before leaving for Concord, Estelle worried, uncharacteristically, about what to wear and how to groom herself, finally settling on a navy-blue dress with white ruffles at the throat, pantyhose, and low-heeled shoes. The time she spent combing her hair seemed drawn out as if she were stoned, and she took even more pleasure than usual in the act, not knowing exactly why, until she remembered her mother used to comb her hair. And yet her memories of childhood were so confused that perhaps it hadn't been Romaine. It might have been one of her aunts or one of the women she called aunts who really weren't relations, or perhaps no one brushed her hair, her memory mere wishful thinking petrified into the appearance of fact by time. In the Jordan kinship, women had babies too early or too late, with so little knowledge of or respect for common family traditions that who was mother and who was daughter often became blurred even in the minds of the women themselves; to very young children, all women were mother and none was mother.

In Tuckerman she stopped at Donald's, bringing the Subaru to the garage to be checked over for the drive.

After Donald finished working on the car, he met her outside for a moment, silent but watching her, his signal he could be spoken to.

"I'm going up to Concord to pay a call on your grandmother Romaine," Estelle said.

Donald took a step backward as if her perfume offended him.

"Fan belt was loose, so I tightened her; freshened your anti-freeze, too." The sun, reflecting off the metallic sheen of Donald's skin, lacerated her eye.

"My, oh, my, I haven't seen her in years." She forced the words.

He made no sign he understood her urgency but he did speak civilly to her.

"They say cars aren't built like they used to be, and they aren't," he said. "They're built better. Especially the engines ... electronic ignitions ... no points to set ... change the oil when you feel like it, though I can't say I recommend that. Anyway, don't worry about this old pig from across the seas. It's engi-neered better than you and me and all the rest of the Jordans in Tuckerman County."

And he showed her his back and strode away.

Before setting out, the Witch bought roses for Romaine but also for her own comfort. She wanted something soft to look at, something soft to smell, something soft to contrast with the metal and glass of the car.

On the road, she imagined cutting her finger on a thorn of a rose bush, and the fragrance from the flowers healed the wound.

The hospital reminded her of the Tuckerman textile mills and shoe shops of decades ago—grim red-brick buildings three and four stories high, at once (it seemed) solid and permanent yet coming apart from the moment they opened. She looked for dazed souls walking the brick pathways; saw none. It didn't dawn on her that two thirds of the buildings were shut down. Rather, she experienced the emptiness of the place as an emptiness in her. A minibus pulled up and half a dozen people got out with the driver, a young woman in tan pants and a sweatshirt. The fact that the driver was a woman, the fact that a woman was in charge, the fact that her dress was casual shocked Estelle. She'd expected all the staff people to wear white uniforms. Before the group disappeared into a building, she was startled by a laugh from one of the patients, startled because the laugh rang with mirth, not madness. Something was wrong. She would have been relieved to hear a howl or a shriek. She sensed she was approaching one of those moments in human life when a belief, so ingrained that it is part of the personality of a person, is proved wrong, dead wrong, wrong from the start.

At the reception desk, she had a panicky moment when the clerk had difficulty finding her mother's name in the files. Finally, she was directed to the geriatrics building. Clutching the bouquet of roses, she made her way down a long hall in the main building. The tile floor was dull and worn from the tramping of countless feet, and yet she saw no people.

Outside, she watched pigeons roost in crannies behind barred windows.

She stopped a bearded man getting into a jalopy that would have made a Jordan teenager proud.

"You work here?" she asked.

"Attendant," the man said.

It occurred to her he might be an escaped patient, stealing a car. The Witch in her searched his eyes for a lie. His eyes said, "I'm tired, I want to go home."

"Where are the crazy people?" she asked.

"Walking the streets," the man said with a faint grin that lightly mocked her question. "Drugs keep them out of the hospitals, that and these new laws."

"Laws?" What could law have to do with mind? she wondered.

"The laws say even if you're crazy the state can't lock you up unless you're dangerous to others or to your own person. People have lost jobs over those laws."

The man drove off, leaving Estelle to mull over whether it was her duty to sound the alarm that a possible mental patient was on the loose.

Unless you're dangerous—the words racketed about in her mind. As far as any Jordan was concerned, everyone was dangerous to everyone else. If danger was the issue, everyone should be locked up. But that wasn't the issue. The issue was crazy people. The reason they were locked up wasn't because they were dangerous or not dangerous but because they were crazy. She could go no further in thinking the matter through, for she had only her Jordan logic to guide her.

Once inside the geriatrics building, she announced herself to a white-uniformed nurse stationed at the reception desk. The woman was about her own age, built like a log skidder, with a scowl that could run a nylon.

"Mrs. Jordan is in Room 202, second floor," the nurse said coldly.

"Do you know my mother?" Estelle asked.

"I've been here twenty-five years, so, yes, I know her, quite well," the nurse said.

Estelle said nothing. She could see now that the nurse had something to say.

"You'd be Estelle," the nurse said.

Estelle returned a bare nod.

"She said if any of her kin came, you'd be the one."

"Is she coherent?"

"Hard to answer that question," the nurse said. "There was a long time that she wasn't coherent, and then she was again. She could have walked out of here ten years ago. She wouldn't leave. This had become her home. Nobody wanted her out

there. And something else—she was afraid. She had about—
oh, I don't know—four or five years of coherence. Today, well,
I couldn't say where she is."

"And the future?"

"Bedridden from physical ailments. As for her mental illness,
you should speak to the doctor."

"But you know what he'll say."

"You're some years too late. She's in her grave, and used to
it." The nurse turned her back on Estelle.

On the walk to her mother's room, Estelle heard moans, a
scream, a cackle, the whispers of professional people. She saw
gaping mouths, bustling help in hospital whites, high-and-
mighty doctors in sport jackets, and, being wheeled down the
corridor, a woman with a withered jaw and only whites for
eyes. These sights and sounds, along with the big nurse's
guard-dog personality, oddly cheered Estelle. She thought, Ah,
this is more like it; the grim expected put her mind at ease.

The unexpected returned when she saw Romaine in bed
looking out the window. She had carried a picture in her mind
of her mother: a big-bodied woman with long black hair, awkward but forceful in her movements. What she saw now was
a frail old woman, thin and dry as the stalks of weeds Estelle
picked.

She reached for a word of love inside herself and, finding
none, held out the flowers.

The old woman slowly removed her gaze from the window
and thrust it nervously toward her daughter, as one attempting
to menace a physically superior opponent with a puny weapon.

"Roses," Estelle said.

Romaine made no move to accept the flowers. Whatever
Romaine was seeing, it was not, strictly, these flowers, another
person, this room. Romaine took in the things around her as
if they were images on a television screen rather than the

evidence of real life. Her eyes roamed from the plain white Johnny gown on her body to the view outdoors (a pine tree, dirty buildings, sky), to the flowers in the hand of her daughter, and finally to Estelle herself.

Her mother's gaze felt like the hand of a spirit passing through her body. Estelle dropped the flowers on the bed, and this act seemed to shake Romaine from her imaginings and moor her to the moment. Something that might have been recognition broke out on her face. Estelle experienced a brief benediction, warmth, as from a light; this—was this the radiance of a mother's love?

"Mother?" The word came hard to Estelle's lips.

The old woman took the longest time to speak. "Estelle? Estelle, can it be you?" she asked, sounding fascinated, yet skeptical too, as if addressing her own echo rising from the depths of a well.

Her mother's voice, unlike the rest of her, had not changed. It was still strung too high, it was still an instrument for digging at her daughter's innards. When she was a girl, most of the time she heard her mother's voice she'd felt fatigued, as if robbed of energy. That same feeling came back now.

"Yes, I'm Estelle."

Romaine turned again toward the window, and spoke as if to someone sitting on the sill, although there was nothing there but bird droppings. "Which one is she? My own Estelle or the other one?"

It was an accusation, delivered in exactly the same tone and with exactly the same quality of mystery that Romaine had used to befuddle her as a child, and Estelle knew no more how to answer it now than she had then.

"I am Estelle," she said.

Romaine paused, and then, as if she had received advice from her invisible counselor, asked slyly, "What has happened to your skin, and around your eyes?"

146

Estelle ran her fingers along the contours of her face. It felt dry, papery; only the bones beneath seemed to have abided over time.

"You're old—my Estelle is not old," Romaine proclaimed like a judge passing sentence.

"Oh, Mommy."

Romaine broke into tears. "Leave me alone. Go away, don't torment me like this."

Estelle tried to understand. Her mother didn't know who she was. Her memory of her was frozen in time.

"It's been so many years, Mommy. I've changed, you've changed. I know I should have come to see you, but..."

Romaine abruptly stopped crying, and pointed a finger at her daughter. "But, dear one, you do come daily to see me. Somebody comes. They say I'm crazy, I make you up, you're a hallucination. We have them on this floor, all the time in the middle of the night, horrible sounds and colors out of nowhere, like an awful pus. But not always—not always. Sometimes what I think I see, I really do see. You. Who are you?"

"I'm Estelle—real—touch me."

"I don't want to; I won't." Romaine buried her face in her hands, and Estelle thought she would weep again. Instead, she peeked at her through the spaces between her fingers like a two-year-old playing a game. "Tell Mommy the truth now. Which Estelle are you?"

Estelle backed a step away from the bed. She was beginning to understand. In her madness and loneliness, Romaine had invented two versions of her eldest daughter, a Witch and a dear self. This was Jordan womanhood: she, the Witch, was a distorted reflection of Romaine; Romaine herself was a distorted reflection of some female figure from the past; and so forth, down through the kinship.

"I am your Estelle," she said.

147

"I don't believe you—you're the other one." Romaine folded her thin arms and sulked.

"Remember, you used to take me with you to pick blueberries. You carried a pail made from a coffee tin. You used to say, 'The poorer the soil, the better the berries.'"

"Oh, how could you know that? We climbed over the granite, you barefoot. No men to beat us, no poverty to wear us down, no kinship—we were free." Romaine immersed herself in the hurt of the memory. "I can't bear this," she said, and turned toward the window.

Estelle knew at that moment that she should have distracted Romaine, kept her away from the hallucination, but something held her back. Finally, she said, "Look at me, Mother," but it was too late.

"Why should it matter which one visits? Whether she brings love or trades in love? It's all the same. Ha-ha-ha-ha!" Romaine's voice, one second sane, in the next mad with laughter, frightened Estelle.

"Mommy," she called, and reached out her hand.

Romaine brushed it away, as if it were an insect, her attention still on the imaginary figure outside the window. "A woman must have love, no matter if it be from the Devil," she said.

"The other Estelle, why does she haunt you?" The Witch was beginning to understand.

"How could it be any other way? I got rid of her."

"That day when Oliver took Estelle away, the other Estelle, took her away in a big car, that was the day, wasn't it?"

Romaine recoiled, not from the question but from the hallucination in the window.

"Tell me," the Witch whispered.

"I sold her," Romaine whispered to the window and then cackled.

She took Romaine roughly by the arm and twisted her toward her so she could look in her eyes. Bits of color in them squirmed like demons in hell. "You sold your daughter to your brother?" she said.

"Not my daughter—the other Estelle. I saved my own Estelle by ridding myself of the other one."

"How much did she fetch?"

"A hundred dollars. Big money in those days." Romaine sounded wistful; she missed the money.

"Knowing Oliver, I bet he offered less," the Witch said. "What took all that time before we went off in the car was the dickering. Isn't that so?"

Romaine pulled away. "How could you know about Oliver? My own Estelle did not know Oliver."

The Witch faced Romaine, and said, "I am the other Estelle."

Back at the front desk, the veteran nurse was on her feet. She'd heard Romaine shriek before. Even now, after all these years, the horror of it troubled her like bad news.

On the return trip to Tuckerman County, the Witch fell into a hole of forgetfulness. She knew, of course, she had visited her mother, knew now what had happened that day Oliver had plucked her from the family shack—"I sold her." And yet she didn't think about any of this as revelation, as instruction, or even as painful information about her past. It seemed trivial. Nothing to get upset about.

It had been a mistake to visit Romaine in the first place, a mistake that she, the Witch, hadn't been responsible for. Mysterious forces had steered her to Concord. Accordingly, what had happened in Corcord was false, a mix-up best put aside. That crazy old woman in the mental hospital was not her mother. Her mother, the woman with the strong hands who had combed her hair, taken her blueberry picking, fended off the menfolk from her, had passed on.

When she returned to Darby that afternoon it had begun to rain; the air was getting colder. Taking in the view from her landing, she felt the seasons change. Soon the green of summer would be gone completely from the hills, the bright colors of fall would vanish. The hills were dark and dreary, merging with the clouds. The north wind blew. The sick don't die in the winter, she thought. They hang on through the cold and snow; suffering itself keeps them alive. When spring comes, and the first warming rays of the sun like loving hands touch their brows, then they die. She longed for the lavender winter sky. She would do Noreen's face today.

Noreen stared up into the diffused glare of the neon lights of the porn shop. Knees together, sitting on the stool behind the counter in her red dress, her right hand reaching upward, with the Witch hovering over her like some mad scientist, Noreen said, "I feel as though I could touch the light."

"It's the toke—it dredges a soul," the Witch said. "You want to touch the light—it means you want to lose yourself in it."

The Witch took a pull on the pipe, inhaling the smoke deep into her lungs, held, and exhaled. She handed the pipe to Noreen, who mirrored the Witch's ritual with the unconscious, slightly askew facility of a child mimicking its elders.

"I never liked pot before," Noreen said. "It always made me feel kind of like—I don't know—I just couldn't enjoy it. But I feel good now, like—I don't know—all shimmery."

She doesn't know what she thinks, what she feels, or who she is, the Witch thought.

"That stuff you smoke from the streets comes from anyplace and it's cut with all manner of disgusting matter—it never smokes the same; your system never gets used to it," the Witch said. "And because it's from someplace else, it makes you a stranger in your own house. But this toke, this is the Witch's homegrown. Good New Hampshire marijuana. It grows from our local wood's soil. You light it, you set free the color of the

150

fall leaves, the taste of the maple sap and the smell of sweet birch. It's got granite in it, too—solid stuff."

She remembered Isaac's lecturing her on the countryside, as if her father truly were an expert and not just a drunk. "There's two kinds of stone rows run through these hills. There's the tight boundary walls the settlers laid up, and then there's wider rows, aiming north; Indians built those for reasons of the spirit, long time before the settlers."

"This pot makes the sound of the rain louder, hurts some— don't you just hate the rain, Estelle?" Noreen shut her eyes, enjoying the touch of the Witch's hands on her face.

"A fall rain is a depressing thing, no doubt," the Witch said. She applied color to the face, puttying over the natural peach glow of it, masking the very thing that moved her. She could hardly bear the sight of the face. She desired at once to tear it to pieces and to weep for its beauty, its goodness, for something beyond her understanding.

After a silence, Noreen said, "Suppose you liked someone and they liked you but they didn't buy you the dress they promised you, and you wanted a VCR, would it be out of line to ask that person to buy you one, if that person could afford it, of course, sort of like to give him the opportunity to show how he really and completely feels about you?"

"You're talking about a product for sale and the price is a VCR," the Witch said.

"No, no," Noreen said. "I'm talking about appreciation; I'm talking about love."

"Appreciation is not worth a VCR, and love is, well... gone." The Witch did not know what to say next. The word *love* had taken her off guard.

"Wouldn't you give a VCR to someone you loved if they wanted it and if you could afford it?" Noreen asked. "He forgot about the dress. But he did get me the CB."

The Witch did not speak. In the silence that followed, Noreen's eyes tripped away from the light, toward some private realm. "I wish, I wish, I wish, I wish." Her words were barely audible.

Where she is now, I too have been, the Witch thought.

"Noreen, are you in love?" The Witch's question snapped Noreen back to the moment.

"I don't know," Noreen said. "When I think I'm in love, it kind of hurts, or maybe I just know it's going to hurt when it's over. Because of me. What I am. With me it's always going to be over, and it's always going to hurt. All I know for sure is I love my children. But the other kind of love, in-love love, like between a man and a woman, I don't know. I do know if I'm not in love, it's like I'm nowhere inside. You, Witch, have you ever been in love?"

"I trade in love," the Witch said. "When you take up pretend love, you hurt at first, then the hurt goes away and you're numb. Soon you realize that right from the start pretend love and real love are the same thing, a trick to keep people breeding. Think about it: you can get as pregnant with pretend love as with real love. In the long run, it doesn't matter how you went about it, as long as you did it, and even that doesn't matter, because even if you don't breed, somebody else will."

Noreen gulped as one shown horrible pictures, subjected to horrible sounds.

"Come on, Noreen, I know you've felt the numbness—no love, but no hurt either." The Witch scraped Noreen with her voice.

"Maybe you're right, maybe I can't feel true love anymore and maybe it doesn't matter anyway," Noreen said. "But I have to keep trying. I need love, real, true love, hurt and all. Do you think somebody will ever truly and forever love me?"

Noreen's passion and sincerity pecked at the heart of the Witch like the beak of a vulture.

At this point, the conversation was interrupted by a banging on the front door of the bookstore.

"A customer—I'm late again opening up." Noreen jumped nimbly from the stool, grabbed the black wig and arranged it on her head.

"Let him stew," the Witch said.

"If Critter finds out, he'll give me holy hell," Noreen said. She skipped over to the entry and pulled the shade up over the window of the door. Through the distorted glass, the Witch recognized the face of the handsome young driver of the Trans Am.

After Noreen let him in, he put a five-dollar bill on the counter and said, "Tokens." She took the money and counted out twenty tokens. The Trans Am kept his hands at his sides so that Noreen put the tokens on the counter for him to take instead of putting them in his hand. Thus, the transaction did not include touch. He wore crisp new blue jeans, a black leather jacket, black boots. From pierced ears hung earrings shaped liked daggers. His blond hair, combed rakishly against the sides of his head, was like water falling from a height. The Witch shifted about, tossed her hair back with a hand, trying to get him to look at her, but his eyes never left Noreen; they roamed along her throat, down to her breasts.

"Noreen." The Witch spoke so the Trans Am could hear the sound of her voice, but he turned for the peep-show booths, and it was as if she did not exist.

"Did I do something?" Noreen was bullied by the Witch's tone.

"Know him?" the Witch whispered now and glanced in the direction of the peep shows.

"Comes in once in a while," Noreen said.

"I bet you'd like to have something like that?"

"I don't know," Noreen grimaced. "I don't like to think about the fellows that come in here. They kind of give me the creeps.

Most of them don't look at you. That one looks you over. I don't like to think about it."

"You're alone here, and there's all this sex leaping out of pages, don't that make you stop and think from time to time?" The Witch wanted to see fear on Noreen's face.

"I don't pay any attention." Noreen stood stiffly, like a child shoved into a corner by an adult.

"You look scared to me."

"You're nice to me and then you pick on me. I don't understand you, Estelle." Noreen was on the verge of tears.

"It'll be all right. I was only teasing," the Witch soothed. She grabbed the broom behind the counter and handed it to Noreen. "Do a little work and you'll feel better."

Noreen left the counter and began to sweep the floor.

The Witch wanted to ask Noreen whether the Trans Am looked at her with more intensity when she wore makeup and the black wig, but of course she knew Noreen could not deal with such a question. While Noreen was busy, the Witch reached under the counter in the shoebox and took one of the girlie pictures Critter had taken of Noreen. Then she said good-bye and left the store. She wasn't exactly sure what she was going to do next; she knew only that she must make contact today with the Trans Am.

She stood outside in the rain by the car. Save for Noreen's Bug, it was the only vehicle in the lot. It had been raining forever, it seemed, and the ground was sopping underfoot. The field grass, which had been so bright and new in midsummer, now was worn, drab, dying. The surrounding forest dripping with rain imprisoned the barn. She could feel no wind, but she could see a nervous fog skitter here and there. Her mind went into a sort of doze. She was aware of everything around her, could have reacted to anyone calling her name. Yet she could not feel the rain, and no thoughts, no memories, no images sprang forth to trouble her; she was empty, insubstantial, a ghost, and almost blissful in her ghostliness.

She didn't know how long she was in the rain, but she was soaked to the skin when the Trans Am came out of the porn shop. He strode toward her, now visible, now obscured by the fog. At moments, it was as if he were walking away from her, but the ground between them was closing, crushing in upon itself, and they were coming together in spite of themselves.

She blocked his way. He looked around. He was going to hit her, she could see, and he wanted to make sure no one would catch him at it. She reached into her bra and handed him the pictures of Noreen. He stepped back, looking at them. The Witch removed her teeth, took off her blouse and bra and flung them aside. Stripped to the waist, her pendulous breasts hanging down, nipples erect, she knelt in the mud beside the car.

The Trans Am knew without hesitation what she was offering. He undid his fly; he was already erect when she went to work on him. He didn't make a sound; he didn't touch her, keeping his hands by his sides. She tried to cup his buttocks in her own hands, but he cuffed them down. If her face brushed his stomach, he pulled away. All he wanted was her mouth. He finished in less than a minute. Then, without a word or a gesture, with no acknowledgment whatever that she existed, he got into his car and drove off, spattering muddy water upon her.

The Witch remained kneeling in the soggy earth, rubbing her nipples between thumb and forefinger, touching herself below with her other hand, marrying tremor to orgasm.

155

12

The Auction

Hadly Blue was surprised by the size of the crowd at the Hillary dairy barn.

"Strange that so many people have turned out for this, when it's doubtful anything will be sold they can use," he said to Persephone Salmon. "I mean Selectman Crabb makes some sense—he's a farmer—but the Jordans? The LaChances? the Achesons? Who among them is going to buy a milk cow?"

"They're here for the same reason we are—theater," Persephone said.

The auction had already started when they arrived. Two men would parade a cow in view, the auctioneer (a fellow with a felt hat and red suspenders) would describe the animal in a language alien to Blue, and the bidding would start. There were perhaps a hundred people standing around or sitting on folding chairs brought in for the occasion, but there were only a dozen or so buyers of bovines. Avalon Hillary sat stiffly in a chair beside the auctioneer. It took Hadly a moment to realize why the farmer looked strange to him. He had exchanged his usual uniform of blue denim overalls for a suit and tie. It was an out-of-date suit, and Hillary seemed uncomfortable in it; the tie was poorly knotted. No one else in the barn wore a suit. Hadly wondered why Hillary had bothered to dress up.

Hadly spotted Critter Jordan and his wife. They had set up

156

a little bar and were selling coffee and doughnuts from the Dunkin' Donuts shop in Tuckerman. The sight triggered Hadley's craving for caffeine along with a hunger for sugar and fat. Yet while he wanted a doughnut he also wanted, by all means, to keep his distance from Critter. Jordan was unlettered if not illiterate, seedy and sneaky, yet oddly likable, at turns intimidating and pathetic, like the hound that followed him everywhere. He stood too close to you when he talked, his breath was bad, and his teeth were worse. He didn't have the built-in social gyroscope of most people. Yet this handicap freed him to speak his mind, while better minds were fettered to convention and etiquette. He was the kind of man who by sheer accident could make a fool of you.

Meanwhile, Critter and Delphina had made twenty-eight dollars thus far selling coffee and doughnuts. Critter was relaxed and pleased with himself until he caught the eye of Professor Hadly Blue. He admired Blue, called him Professor Had or Doc. But there was something mysterious, strange, disturbing about him. Once, Critter had recited to him the only poetic lines he knew, "*Roses are red, violets are blue, If I had a face like you, I'd join a zoo.*" Professor Had had blinked, then grinned like a maniac. People with too much education were uncomfortable to have around because you couldn't know what they were thinking, any more than Crowbar here, dozing at his feet, could know what his master was thinking. Why'd Professor Had come to this auction? To laugh at us hicks? Critter kicked Crowbar.

"What he do?" Delphina asked.

"Nothing," Critter said. "I let him have it on general principles. You suppose Professor Had over there will be buying a cow?"

"He's already wangled himself some mighty impressive stock in the widow Salmon," Delphina said.

They giggled together.

ERNEST HEBERT

Of recent, Critter and his wife were getting along. Why, it had gotten so he found himself preferring her company to the company of male kin. The idea that a man could be friends with his wife was strange to him, and he was a little afraid of it. Yet it felt so good, so sweet. Was this what life was about: love for children, friendship with your woman, sex life half in bed, half in your head? Critter sighed, half in contentment and half in fear, thinking about Noreen.

Delphina had to know something was up, and yet she hadn't said anything, hadn't hinted around, hadn't done anything but be his friend, the mother of his children, the queen of his domain. He wished he could talk to her about it, explain to her that he loved her and that he was happy with her, that Noreen actually solidified their marriage. How could you say to a wife, "This piece I got on the side takes the restlessness out of me, and so now I'm not cranky, and I'm happy to be a family man. If she goes, you'll suffer."

"Want a doughnut?" he asked.

"Already had three," Delphina said.

"I can remember when I was a kid, I'd dream about dough-nuts." Critter saw those doughnuts now, parading from his memory past the front porch of his consciousness: jelly dough-nuts with round smiling faces, marching on chorus-girl legs with mesh stockings. His father would buy the doughnuts at Doris's Bakery in Tuckerman. (It had closed down only re-cently.)

"Crullers, or what?" Delphina asked.

"Jellies, big fat ones, oozing sticky red jelly," Critter said.

"Nobody's perfect," Delphina said. Then she added, "Critter, I was going to wait, but there's something I've been meaning to talk to you about."

More than the words themselves, the shift in her tone set off a fire bell in Critter's mind. *Ding-dong!* She knows! Here it comes—the crack of doom.

"I was talking to Noreen Cook the other day." Delphina's eyes narrowed. My gosh, Critter thought, how strong, mean, and unforgiving a woman can be.

He'd deny everything. Noreen Cook, that scrawny bitch— think better of me than that. No, that was no good. He'd say it only happened once—a one-shot deal. That wouldn't work. He'd say it was Noreen's fault, she put him up to it. No, that was too low, even for him. Still, a man had to do what he had to do. It didn't matter what he said, Delphina would never believe him. He'd have to tell the truth, admit his guilt. I done it, I was wrong, I'll never do it again, I love you more than anything else in the world, more than Crowbar, more than my van, more than the kids. I promise, I promise, I promise. He was beginning to feel an odd sense of relief creeping into his anxiety. Delphina would forgive him. He could be himself again. Wouldn't have to live a lie. Everything was going to be all right.

"So what?" Critter said.

Delphina did not respond. She was distracted by some activity toward the front. Critter peered into the barn gloom, which was cut only slightly by a string of temporary lights.

"Look at her, ain't she something to be behold," Delphina said. Critter's eyes came to rest on a cow. He recognized the beast. He'd worked briefly a few years back for farmer Hillary and this was his super breeder. They were getting ready to auction her off. He wondered vaguely whether Delphina was going to bid on the cow. In fact, however, Delphina had not noticed the cow. Her admiring eyes were for Natalie Acheson, one of the rich ladies of Upper Darby.

"She smells like all the rest," Critter said, wondering whether to be grateful to the cow for staying his execution or whether he should press Delphina for her accusations and get them over with.

"Oh, no," Delphina tittered. "She wears special perfume they get from New York or India or someplace like that. I know, I smelled her."

"A high-class cow is still a cow," Critter said.

Delphina poked Critter in the side. "Sometimes, you are about the funniest man I know."

He wanted then to tell Delphina the one about the hunter who was bit by a snake in the privates. Hunter named Reb was taking a leak when a big snake bit him you know where. His friend Rab ran twelve miles to town for help, but Doc Jones (maybe he'd call him Doc Blue in the story) was busy delivering Mrs. MacIntosh's baby. "Reb's been bit by a snake," says Rab. "What manner of snake?" Doc Blue asks. "Black snake with a red stripe," Rab says. "You've got to suck out the poison," Doc says. "And if I don't?" Rab asks. "Then Reb will surely die," Doc says. So Rab runs the twelve miles back to his fallen friend. Over hill and dale, through swamp and forest he goes. He arrives, and Reb is barely breathing. He whispers to Rab, "What did the doc say? What did he say?" Rab answers, "He says you're going to die." Surely, this joke would put Delphina in a good mood. As Critter was mulling over this possibility, he listened to himself blurt out, "I can't stand the suspense any longer. What's your problem with Noreen?"

"It's not with Noreen, it's with you," Delphina said, and her eyes narrowed again. "I heard at Tammy's that you put a CB in Noreen's car. You never did that for me."

"Is that all you want—a CB?"

"In the Caddy,'" Delphina said. "This may not be important to you, but it's important to me."

As Delphina's words sunk in, Critter spontaneously leaped to his feet and laughed aloud. A second later he was surprised to find himself eyeball-to-eyeball with Hadly Blue.

"What's up, Doc?" he shouted with glee. He swept up a doughnut and stuck it under Blue's nose. "Here you go, Doc— for you, free."

"No, thank you; no, thank you; no, thank you," Blue said, moving off, vanishing into the crowd.

The noise level in the barn fell then, and the attention of Critter and Delphina turned toward the auction block. What had quieted the spectators was the bidding on Hillary's supercow. It was sky-high—out of sight. When it was over, someone began to clap. Others followed. Soon everyone was cheering. The cow got a standing ovation.

Critter watched the old farmer remove his tie and let out a whoop, like from an old Western movie. Critter could see there was more to Hillary's elation than just the money, but what it was he did not know, only that Hillary had something at this moment he didn't have, and likely never would.

It was two days after Avalon's cow auction that the Witch again made contact with the Trans Am. She met him outside in the parking lot of the auction barn.

"Do me," he said.

"Not now," she said.

"Here—now," he said.

"Later, when it's dark. On the road, while you're driving fast. I want to be in the car, and I want it to be going fast, a hundred miles an hour."

He considered, staring off into the gray sky.

"I'll bet you never got your rocks off at a hundred miles an hour," she said.

"These country roads are no good for that. We'll cross over onto the interstate. I'll punch it past a hundred, way past, and you can do me." He spoke, she could see, as though her suggestion had been part of his plans all along. She noted this attempt at deception, the fact that she hadn't been deceived, as a weakness. I'm smarter than he is, she thought.

The moon was up when she met him on the highway. She slid into the seat beside him. The engine growled, tires squealed, and they were launched. The Trans Am lounged on Route 21 five miles below the speed limit. They were fifteen minutes away from I-91.

The anticipation of speed and sex stirred the tremor in her. She teased herself with it, bent inward to it, then extended herself outward from it, so she could almost see her breath deepen, as if she were watching the emotions of a woman about to dive into the sea from the top of a cliff. She was, she thought, in love with the Trans Am, even while she understood that this affirmation spat in the face of love. She could not feel love; he could not feel love; together, they could not feel as lovers. They could not make love; they could only mock love; theirs was a death mask of love.

Now they were crossing the bridge over the Connecticut River. Free of the partial arch of trees, the road opened for a moment to the sky. Moonlight seemed to seep into the car. The Witch looked down into the river. Crooked lines of light traced the shore. The light defined the river; the light said, "The river is alive, dark, and serious in its business as a pumping heart."

The Witch turned her eyes to the Trans Am. The moonlight was a blue-white stocking pulled over his features. Like a huge and terrible cat, he seemed at once about to doze off and to spring to action. The light could say nothing about him. He obscured the light.

In a minute after crossing the bridge, they reached the interstate and the Trans Am headed north. He turned off the cassette player and said, "Listen." He wanted her to hear the sounds of the gathering speed of the automobile.

As it went faster and faster, her connections with the familiar parted like colored threads fluttering in some magical, windblown light. The highway rose into the sky, the Trans Am with it. For a few minutes, they didn't speak or touch or look at one another. Even the sound of their breath was lost in the moan of speed. Perhaps at this moment they *were* lovers. She felt about him as she used to feel about small wooden objects Oliver used to carve—crude heads, animals, crests, sometimes only shapes. In them he had left his softness, the softness that held her in bondage to him as sure as the hardness did. She would hold the carvings to her bosom in order to bring herself the comfort Oliver the man no longer brought, while at the same time she would entertain herself with visions of burning them. In the conflict of these two emotions, she could feel her womanhood divide in two.

The Trans Am reached into her blouse and squeezed her breasts, gently at first, then more violently. He squeezed until she whimpered a little with pain, then he released her. He's got a nose for death and no conscience, she thought. He says to himself, If I want it, it must be good; if I don't, it's no good. He's simple and unwholesome—he's what I want, what I need. She unzipped his jacket and pants, exposing a V of bare flesh from throat to crotch. She kissed his chest and ran her hands over his body.

She enjoyed his physique under her fingertips. It reminded her of the car itself—smooth and hard. His chest was almost hairless, and there was a hint of baby fat on his hips and under his chin. She guessed that as a boy he'd been chubby, matured late, almost overnight becoming a roaring man, and his idea of himself hadn't quite caught up to the fact of his body. The blond curly hairs rose from between his legs like field grass. She liked the Johnny-jump-up quality of his pecker, so different from the crank-jobs of her old men. (She lingered for a moment over a thought of aging sailors hoisting anchor.)

"Take your teeth out," the Trans Am said.

She did as she was told, then lay the side of her face against his shoulder and watched the road. She could feel the tenseness in him, which was the tenseness of the metal of the car under the stress of speed. They passed a pickup truck pulling

163

a horse trailer. There was something about it, blinking and blurring, that puzzled and disoriented her until she realized she was traveling faster than she ever had in her life, seeing the world as never before.

The Trans Am glanced at her. His eyes were bright but impersonal. He ran a hand across her forehead, down the back of her neck; he stroked her palms. He was trying to feel signs of fear in her; fear was like food to him and he was hungry. But there was no fear in her. Her skin was dry as dead grasses.

He grabbed her by the hair, shook her head for a moment, then shoved it down to his loins. The darkness, the moistness, the vibrations of the car meeting air, the tires burning on the highway: these sensations interwound like snakes with the tremor. When it seemed as if the car would shake apart from the speed, he came.

They drove on, plunging northward at a hundred and thirty miles an hour. When the Trans Am wasn't looking, the Witch returned the teeth to her mouth.

"I feel like a beer," the Trans Am said.

"What do you drink?" she asked.

"Molson Golden Ale—nothing else," he said.

"Canadian stuff."

The Trans Am said nothing.

"Let's go to Canada, get the real thing," the Witch said.

"Canada—you're crazy." He smiled, as one scorning a fool. And yet they would head for Canada, she knew. He had no imagination, she could see; he could be steered here and there, and never quite realize it.

They didn't slow until they approached the border. Signs warned them they were leaving the United States. The Witch didn't exactly believe them. She knew of course there was such a place as Canada. She knew some basic geography. The world was round, covered mainly with water. There were continents; there were countries, zillions of them, populated by zillions of people, many of them who had no shoes to wear or who were communists. Yet while she knew all this to be more or less true, something in her didn't believe her knowledge. Something in her said the physical universe was limited to Tuckerman County. Everyplace else was a dream, a hallucination. A real place, insofar as it had meaning to her, had somehow to be linked with the county. She could believe in New Hampshire and almost believe in Massachusetts, Vermont, even Maine, because these places seemed like an extension of Tuckerman County. Connecticut, New York, states farther west and south dissolved into a mist of geographical knowledge, newscasts, hearsay. Canada hardly seemed on the same planet. Yet here they were: Canada.

When they crossed the actual borderline, she didn't so much expect things to look different—an ocean, strange buildings, men on horseback—but rather that she would feel different. Outside of herself, thrilled perhaps. But for the moment she felt the same as before. She was who she was, Canada was what it was, like Vermont, which was what it was, like Tuckerman County. The Witch was disappointed.

Up ahead, lights flashed in warning or welcome. Hard to tell which. A few seconds later, a sign glowered—and they were slowing to be checked at a border stop. This was more like it, this was foreign. A guard in uniform, hands behind his back, peered into the car as he addressed the Trans Am.

"What is your nation of citizenship?" he asked.

"USA," the Trans Am said after hesitating.

"New Hampshire," the Witch said.

"What is your purpose in visiting Canada?" the guard asked.

"Vacation," the Trans Am said.

"What will be the length of your stay?"

"Two weeks," the Trans Am said.

165

The guard waved them on.

He spoke with a Frenchy accent. The Witch liked that, not knowing why.

The Trans Am was pleased with the lies he had told, the Witch could see. He was the type that was more comfortable with falsehood than truth. Like herself, he knew a truth, even a seemingly harmless truth, exposed the teller of it. It was always best to lie when you could get away with it.

I-91 became Route 55, the highway marker decorated with a picture of a maple leaf. This, the Witch could see, had something to do with Canada as an idea, although for the life of her she couldn't nail down the exact meaning. What was so great about maple leaves, and what could they have to do with an entire country? Road signs were written in French and English, and this too didn't make sense to her. Why couldn't these people settle on one language? If you spoke two languages, which language did you think in? This one or that one? Both? Were you a different person in French than you were in English?

"Ain't you glad you don't talk French," she spoke aloud to herself.

"I do speak French. They made you learn it in one of the schools I was sent to," the Trans Am said.

Confusion of language: maybe that was his problem, the Witch thought.

"You went to a lot of schools?" she said.

"I ran away from most of them. One day they didn't catch me."

"On his own in the cruel world," the Witch said.

"I did all right. Did some dealings." His face didn't reveal the lie, but his hands did. They tightened on the steering wheel. In the future, she wouldn't tease him unless deliberately to provoke him.

A boy loose on the streets, men on the lookout for such

boys—his story was clear to the Witch. He was like her, a whore—wounded, dangerous, itchy for revenge.

They turned off the highway at the first good-size town, Magog. The stores had closed, so no Molson. Before the Trans Am could work up an anger, the Witch spotted twinkling lights that signaled a tavern.

It seemed to the Witch that the bar was more colorful, more cheerful, more refined than the bars she was accustomed to. Otherwise it was simply a bar—men full of har-har-har, a pool table, the bartender a woman, a young floozy wearing tight pants.

"Molson Golden Ale," ordered the Trans Am.

"Canada Dry ginger ale," ordered the Witch.

The Trans Am sampled the brew, then took a long drink. She watched him eye the floozy's rear end. He smacked his lips. Moist, they seemed vaginal to the Witch.

"You like that?" The Witch pointed to the floozy with her eyes.

"I'd like to beat her ass," he said.

"On the drive back, when I'm taking care of you, think about it." The Witch put her hand on his thigh.

"It's a good car—old, but solid and well cared for. I'll guarantee that, since I did the caring," Avalon said, as he opened the passenger door for Estelle. Since the cow auction, he was more restless than ever but also happier, almost giddy. He was on the brink of big changes, she could see.

They eased out onto River Road, rolling easily. Never drove over fifty with a woman in the car, he'd said. Estelle felt herself fall into a calm. She imagined she'd learned to swim and lay floating on her back on a warm lake, watching clouds frolic as if the sky were a big stage.

"This car is the only mechanical contrivance I ever babied," Avalon said. "I rust-proofed the body every two years, and just this spring I had it repainted. Goddamn acid rain raises hell with a finish nowadays. Whitewall tires—nothing but the best for this old girl. I've changed the oil with the rise of every moon since I bought her—new, zero miles on her, virgin. I won't say the year. And she's only got thirty-five original thousand miles on her."

He wasn't the kind of man who could say right out that he liked a woman. He found it easier to express his affection by talking about a thing. So Estelle listened, as one dreamily contemplating an admirer sing her praises. Never mind that he was talking about the car. She knew the affection was for her, and she was pleased.

"Fact is," he went on, "I don't have any actual necessity for this vehicle. As my father was fond of saying, 'A farmer can tell himself he needs a pickup truck, and the Lord will forgive him for browning the truth a little.' But a car? A big car at that? Noooo. A car is an out-and-out sin of luxury in a world weighed down with poverty. That's why I love it so."

They crossed the Connecticut River. Estelle could feel the emptiness between the bridge and river. He was taking her to dinner in Vermont. He wasn't ashamed to be seen in public with her, just uneasy about the situation. Perhaps this was because it wasn't the town he wanted to shock, so much as the ghosts of his ancestors. As far as the town was concerned, he didn't want the people to think anything about him one way or the other. So he was more comfortable hiding her from their eyes.

"Why don't you turn that farm of yours into a used-car lot?" she suggested.

"You think I have an aptitude for salesmanship, do you?" He was amused.

"Oh, you're full of that stuff you shovel to make the grass grow."

Avalon chuckled. "Sell cars," he said, tickled by the logic of the idea, so near to yet so distant from the Hillary heart. "You're quite a kidder, Estelle. Quite a kidder. Instead of cows grazing in the field, we'll park cars in them. Instead of a barn, we'll have a garage. Instead of cowshit under my shoes, I'll have ...well, I don't know—new shoes."

Before the auction he'd complained constantly about the work load of the farm. Now, after the stock had been sold and taken away, he complained the other way. Time on his hands, nothing to do, a feeling of strangeness, especially when he looked at the land—empty. So he pestered her with his presence. They took rides; they went out to eat; anything to get away from the farm and do something. She loved his company, maybe even loved the man himself. She didn't know. It seemed to her that one of the rules for a long life of the spirit was: Be grateful for a feeling but don't trust it. But what did you do when you weren't sure what the feeling was?

"If I've learned anything it's that I've carried a chip on my shoulder against my father and grandfather, and I suppose I sold the herd to spite the past, but darned if I could go so far as to asphalt the fields and park cars on them," he said.

"Sell it—everything," Estelle said.

"I don't want to sell. I'll tell you, Estelle, I like grass. I like to watch it grow, I like to watch the butterflies spring from it—though I admit I cut down on the population by mowing the cocoons as I mowed for hay. You understand, the farm always came first."

"Uh-huh."

In her mind's eye, Estelle could see a white house with lots of shelves where you set down weed pots of wood and pottery, earthen objects, containers for ribbons and all sorts of interesting things, a library of books packed with pressed flowers and leaves.

There was a pause. He was thinking about her *uh-huh*. "You don't like your grass green," he said.

"I like it dried, as you know," she said.

"I never met a woman like you—don't like growing things. The women I've known..."

"Farm women—what do you expect?"

"Uh-huh," he mimicked her, and they both laughed.

His car *was* solid, she thought. It was like a bunker. But bunkers never worked. The enemy went around, or tossed grenades through the windows, or the people inside went nuts from their own company.

"Pitiable," she said, after a pause, speaking a thought.

"Who—old farmers?"

"The human race."

"Work, worry, breed, die," Avalon said, and they tasted the sweetness of a moment of shared philosophy.

They arrived at the restaurant, the Fife and Drum. She'd always wondered what a fife was, but it had never occurred to her to seek out the answer. It was one of those trivial questions that pester a mind over a lifetime without that mind ever putting it to rest.

"Before we go in, I got something for you." Avalon's voice was suddenly gruff. "I was going to wait until I brought you home, but if I don't get this over with now, it'll ruin my supper."

He opened the trunk of the Buick. The inside was spotless save for a brown paper bag. He opened the bag and peeked in.

"You keep this," he said, so gruff now he would have sounded angry to a passerby.

She took the bag and looked inside. There was a potted plant in it.

"My wife kept plants like some people keep fish or *National Geographic* magazines," he said. "When she died, I gave 'em all away. Too much bother they were. Well, this one escapes me. It was in the bathroom on the windowsill behind the curtain. I'd never noticed. Who knows how many years it had been there. When I finally discovered it, it was almost dried out to death. Well, I been taking care of it and I don't much like the work. So I'm giving it to you. Put it in the trash for all I care. It isn't worth anything. It's not the plant I'm giving, it's a piece of my past."

So this is love, Estelle thought. He offers, she accepts. Afterward, she has, he has not. She watches it grow, he searches for what he lost. From this, things are made, wars instigated, babies born. The race is preserved, held together by a vague and probably false idea of the past.

Avalon stepped back, seeing a change in her eyes.

Estelle understood the gift of the plant. It was his first move in courtship. Soon he'd be asking her to change her address to River Road. He'd say, as old man Williamson had said, "A lot of people our age live together—never mind the matrimony." He was asking for comfort. Ferrying old men to the grave: it was her lot in life. No denying the pattern over the years. No denying that if she moved in with him, he'd die, and afterward she'd feel an odd sense of victory. Triumph would replace what had passed as love.

"I don't want it," she said, handing him the bag.

He looked at her, to make sure she had understood the purpose behind his act. "I thought you were my girl," he said.

She said nothing. When he looked again into her eyes, he saw the Witch's brew in them.

"You got things to do, have you?" he said.

"In a manner of speaking," she said.

"Well, why don't you do them and get back to me?"

"Because you won't want me then," the Witch said.

"Oh, come on."

171

"Only reason you want me now is to piss on the graves of your fathers," she said. "But never mind, when this is done, I doubt I'll want you."

Avalon laughed bitterly, ironically. He knew this was the end of them. "Can't you tell an easy lie?" he said.

"If I have to," the Witch said.

13

Preparations for the Shedding of Blood

As usual, they eased west on Route 21, the cassette player blaring, then rocketed north on the interstate. They said little; they were from different worlds, had nothing to talk about. And anyway he didn't like her to talk, didn't like talk in general, or silence, or peaceful-type music; he wouldn't abide anything that disturbed his pleasure, a union of music, motion, and metal, produced, she understood, by the car, by the leather he wore against his skin, by the knife strapped to his leg, and by a lowly old whore.

One thing that attracted her to him was that he was the opposite of a Jordan. His teeth were beautiful, straight, white, cared for. His clothes seemed perpetually new. He was always clean and clean-shaven. He had money, yet he seemed to hold no job. He gave the impression money came his way, so there was little reason to give it any thought. His valuables consisted of his car, his anger, and his erection—a thing, a feeling, a force. He had never mentioned his name or where he lived or who his loved ones were. The very idea of loved ones was alien to him. She knew who he was, of course, a Butterworth from Upper Darby, living with his mother, Mrs. Acheson, yet she refused to think of him as a person; he remained the Trans Am to her.

When the car began to shake with speed, seemed on the

verge of disintegration, she removed her teeth and placed them discreetly on the seat beside her so he would not see them. She bent to him, then, laboring at her craft. Afterward, they would stop at a convenience market and buy some Canadian ale. They'd come back to Darby along the river, the old road, traveling slowly, he drinking, she smoking her pipe: it was only then she'd wish he'd turn down the loud music and say something.

It took only a minute or so before she sensed his entire body begin to stiffen—even his blood went rigid. She anticipated his orgasm, a cry like a lost boy's. A moment later, she tasted the first warm jet of semen.

But at the same time, she was startled by a screeching sound coming from the car itself. Her mind flashed back to the day off River Road, when the Trans Am had shrieked in anger and pain. I was right, she thought now, a man and his machine become a third thing. A split second later, the Trans Am's foot hit the brake. The Witch felt herself thrown forward, jamming her shoulder against the dashboard pad. The Trans Am grabbed her hair and pulled her to a seated position beside him.

"Fuzz Buster went off! Speed trap ahead!" He shouted in anger.

The Witch reached for her teeth. They were gone, apparently sent flying by the sudden deceleration of the car.

The Trans Am shut off the radar warning device and continued to brake rhythmically, easing off at fifty-five as they passed a state trooper car parked behind some trees on the median strip.

"Ruined my cum! Ruined it!" The Trans Am shook his fist at her, as if it had been her fault. For a moment, the Witch thought he would burst into tears.

Like a panicked blind woman, the Witch continued to feel along the seat beside her for her teeth, finally finding them in the crack between seat and door. Usually she slipped them back into her mouth with great secrecy and care. But she was frantic now, and she shoved them in just as the Trans Am returned his eyes to hers. In his eyes she saw her tremor flame up, die, and from the ashes flame up again, all new and strange, then flicker and go out, extinguished by an unfelt wind. She sifted through the ashes. They were cold. She hurt inside, and the hurt was like a hard embrace, and then there was no hurt, there was nothing. Love cauterizes the wound that it inflicts, she thought. The tremor was no more than a tiny fire now, a discomfort instead of a desire. She could smell something like candles burning at a funeral. Estelle is dying, she thought. I smell her skin smolder.

"I need an ale," the Trans Am said, and the car dipped into the Springfield, Vermont, exit ramp.

She could not tell whether her sadness was true. This feeling: Is it mine, yours, ours together, some graver thing? If I bend to it, will it save us?

She wanted to speak, to midwife the thought into meaning with words, but of course she said nothing. She stilled herself, body and mind, as one at the sickbed of a friend. The Trans Am remained silent, his face sullen, muscles tensed.

They stopped at a gas station, an old place spruced up into a convenience market. The Trans Am sent her in to buy the usual six-pack.

She returned with a bag cradled in her arm. He didn't even wait until she shut the door before peeling out of the lot. The smell of burning candles vanished, replaced by the smell of tires burning on asphalt. They were on the road again, riding the slithery snake that is Route 5 in Vermont. He handed her the opener from the glove box, and she took the cap off the bottle.

He grabbed the beer, drank—and grimaced.

"What's this?" His voice accused.

"Molson's."

"This is Molson beer. I drink the ale, Molson Golden Ale."

"What difference does it make?" she asked.

"It makes no difference at all," he said, in a warm, affectionate tone, the timbre of which she had not heard in years but which she knew how to react to. She threw up a hand to protect her face.

The bottle of beer, which the Trans Am had swung backhandedly in the general direction of her head, hit her forearm, glanced off her temple and toppled onto the car seat. The soft flesh of the side of his palm lingered for a second against her face. The Witch bit the hand.

The Trans Am pulled away at the first pain and jerked the teeth right out of the Witch's mouth. The dentures remained clamped in his hand. His face contorted, as if he'd discovered leeches sucking him, the Trans Am shook the dentures from his hand. They dropped to the floor at her feet.

She picked them up and held them in her hands, as a child might hold a baby chick.

Something in her shouted danger—but too late. This time the Trans Am hit her directly on the cheekbone with the back of his closed fist. She knew what was coming next. A man beats you, and he gets angrier blow by blow because you remind him how low he is. He reacts by blaming you. Later, he says, "What's a woman for but to help a man find relief?" And you say, "Sure, I get it." Now you both have a reason for him to beat you. Before she felt the pain of the blows, she felt the fear in her belly. She was not afraid to die or even to suffer; what she feared was mutilation. She tried to protect first her face, then her breasts. A beating wasn't so bad when a man was very drunk because he'd tire quickly. But when he was sober, or after he'd only had a couple, he could go on forever, it seemed, until there was nothing left of you but something that looked run over.

The next blow did not hurt. It took a second for her to figure out why. She was outside herself, suspended somewhere above the car, deep into the night, and yet able to see into the car. Curled and stiff at the far edge of the passenger seat lay Estelle. And she returned to her body again; she *was* Estelle, feeling the hurt, falling into the rhythm of the Trans Am administering the beating. Threes and twos, three blows, followed by two breaths—*Smack! Smack! Smack! Um-poof! Um-poof!* Hit, hit, hit, breathe, breathe. *Smack! Smack! Smack! Um-poof! Um-poof!* Everything has its beginning in pain and rhythm. I am the beginning, Estelle thought.... And she was again the Witch, counting, calculating. *Smack!* (one), *smack!* (two), *smack!* (three). Before the *um-poof* of the first released breath, the Witch uncoiled and struck, going for his eyes.

They battled. The Witch had the advantage now. The Trans Am wanted to live. He had to try to hold the car on the road while he kept her off him. She managed to interpose herself between the windshield and his eyes. The car leaned to one side, skidding on two wheels, the sound of it like some strange bird searching for home from a point far above land. She was that bird. She could feel, almost to the point of enjoyment, the car slice toward what seemed like the edge of the horizon. She heard the Witch in herself shout the word "Die," the voice harsh, angry. *Be calm, accept your fate, love those who mean you harm. Dying this way, so full of event but without meaning, like birthing a child that has no heartbeat, is a fit end for the Witch, but not for Estelle. If I should die again, if I should die again, if I should die again...*

The moment passed. The Trans Am shoved her aside enough to regain his view of the road and command of the steering wheel. The car settled back down on four tires and drifted toward the shoulder of the road, more or less under control.

Once they came to a stop, they wrestled until the Witch was

sprawled on the seat, the Trans Am astride her, holding her wrists. A car passed, its headlights illuminating the Trans Am's face. It was radiant, like a candlelit statue of a saint.

She stopped struggling, staring at his face for the longest time. He squatted over her, immobile, indecisive; finally, he released her.

"We could have been killed, smashed—really killed." He proclaimed a mystery. His face glowed from the inside.

"We're saved," the Witch said.

"Saved," he said.

They had sex right there, for the first time conventional intercourse.

Afterward, he was almost tender, wiping her face with his handkerchief, as if it could wipe away bruises.

They started back. She was thirsty, so he gave her one of the beers. She lit her pipe, took a pull and handed it to him. Continuing on the road, traveling very slowly, they shared the drink and they shared the toke.

He was, she thought, the kind of fellow who had to feel high to feel anything. And yet he couldn't make himself high. He had to take a drug, or somebody else had to do it for him, or events had to come together accidentally and stun him. He was unhappy, but he didn't know he was unhappy, at least not in so many words, because he'd always been unhappy and so had nothing to compare unhappiness to. He mistook highs for happiness. He was, she thought, the perfect lover for such as her.

By the time they crossed into New Hampshire, the Witch had begun to feel her bruises. She'd protected her face fairly well. It was sore, and it would be swollen and discolored in the morning, but the skin wasn't broken. One ear hurt, and it was hot to the touch. A rib felt funny, as if it was loose, although it didn't give her much pain, and she could breathe all right. Mainly, her arms and shoulders ached from taking most of the blows. She didn't feel nauseated. Usually, after Oliver beat her, she'd wanted to throw up. The pain, taken as a whole, was almost comforting. It screened minor annoyances such as the boredom of driving, the discomfort of loud music; it allowed her to concentrate on her thoughts.

From the start there had been no love in her to give; from the start there had been a Witch in her. She had survived on the belief that she had loved Oliver; yet she had triumphed over him by denying the possibility of love. What troubled her now was a vague feeling of incompleteness accompanied by a craving for love, in the full knowledge she could never have it. Avalon had taught her that. If she could destroy that need, she might be free of it. And then in a vision enhanced by toke and fatigue, she was seeing Noreen. The lettering on her red dress said "I" AM LOVE. She returned her attention to the Trans Am. Even in calmness, anger shone from him.

"I want to touch your face," the Witch said.

"I don't like to be touched."

"A world of hurt builds up in you, doesn't it?" she said.

"Stay clear from my face," he said.

They drove on in silence. A few minutes later, the Trans Am said, "Bring your hand up real slow."

With exaggerated caution, the Witch raised her hand to his face. His cheeks were smooth, and there was a curve where his chin parted in the middle. His lips felt like roses on her fingertips. She sensed the moment when he could bear this intimacy no longer and she dropped her hand to her side.

"When you get pent up, you always have to hurt somebody, and is it always a woman?" the Witch probed.

The Trans Am said nothing.

"After you hurt them, you feel sick or anything?"

"I feel good, I feel relieved." She could feel the threat in his voice.

"Beforehand, you worry you'll hurt somebody?" she asked.

179

"Not exactly."

"You worry about losing control, making a mistake, getting caught. Tell me if I'm wrong," the Witch said.

The Trans Am wavered between continuing the conversation, which was unburdening him, and ending it because it was exposing him. He understood she wasn't afraid of him for the simple reason that she didn't care what happened to her. Perhaps he'd had a moment or two like that, and he knew the freedom it brought, the power. He was jealous of this power. She could steer him here and there, because he coveted this power. If she should ever weaken and he read fear on her face, he would have the power and she would be destroyed.

"What do you want?" he asked.

"Listen close," the Witch said. "I can help you find what *you* want."

He said nothing, but he listened intently.

"Young, scared, alone—I can make it easy for you," the Witch said.

The Witch lived like a robot, programmed by some mastermind long since gone by. She prepared her meals, she kept her house, she satisfied her customers, she engaged in small talk, she drove her car. But she felt curiously detached from these activities. They were not her life; they were duties carried out to oblige a being different from the one that inhabited her soul. There, in that dark keep, she lived; there she plotted. She wanted—had to—destroy Noreen Cook, to save herself. But she didn't know why. She nourished herself by the compulsion to get on with the dirty business at hand; only the question— why—confused her. Why? No sense looking for answers, any-more than there was sense in looking for the answer to, why the seasons, why the moon? She understood this much: for something to be born, something has to die. There was one too many of her.

She tried to reason out her troubles, and that process only increased her confusion. If, as she believed she must, she destroyed Noreen, she would destroy herself, for Noreen was a part of herself. But that didn't make sense; the idea of sense itself didn't make sense: the ability to reason was a curse for a creature, like carrying a useless horn on top the head. Ideas, images, sounds, memories came and went from her mind like pedestrians on a busy street. She couldn't put them in any order, couldn't make sense of them. Thoughts of Romaine visited her often. Crazy old woman: Are you this one, my own, or the other one? She had to forgive Romaine—she had to get even with Romaine.

Over and over again, a truth sounded inside her: somebody has to die, somebody has to die, Noreen has to die. *Not Noreen—anybody but Noreen.* Possible subjects paraded before her mind like characters in a police lineup from an old television show. Herself? Noreen—no, not Noreen? The Trans Am? Both of them, Noreen and the Trans Am? A stranger? Someone she loved, whose death would bring on her own? Avalon? Donald? Who's guilty here? One? All?

The Witch read about Aronson's death in the *Tuckerman Crier.* His picture was on the front page. He was in a flower shop, buying roses for his wife, when two men attempted to rob the place at knifepoint. Aronson pulled his pistol, disarmed the men, and held them to await the police. But one of the men, only eighteen and apparently strung out on drugs, began to advance toward him. Aronson warned the man to keep back, but he kept coming. Aronson held his fire, and the man attacked him. In the struggle that followed, the gun went off. The bullet exploded in Aronson's lungs and ruptured the aorta. Bystanders called Aronson a hero.

The hero was survived by his wife, one son, and one daughter. The Witch hadn't known Aronson had children, knew practically nothing about his family except that his wife had an aversion to oral sex. To conclude her business with Aronson, the Witch felt it necessary to see his wife, the son, the daughter; thus she considered the funeral as an opportunity. She didn't want them to know who she was, their loved one's whore, but she did want them to notice her; she wanted something of her, her witchness, to bend into their memories. She dressed in black and purple, wearing a veil to obscure her face.

The funeral was held in a new church on the Tuckerman flats. When she thought of this area, she visualized the way it was thirty years ago—cornfields and treeless swamp and expansive sky, open, between the density of the city and the density of forested hills beyond. Now, filled in, it was crowded with streets, houses, apartment buildings, a shopping center. The changes, the fact that she couldn't reconcile herself to them, made her experience the strangeness in herself as a lost moment in time, as if she herself didn't exist except as somebody's memory, probably defective, of a place, an idea.

The church was of red brick, with a roof held up by huge wooden beams of sandwiched lumber. Oak pews stained blond pleased the eye and the hand. The brick, bare and unadorned, left the Witch believing the church was still in the process of construction. The matter puzzled her, for certainly the interior would look better with some kind of paneling. Perhaps the congregation was waiting for Christ to return and decorate the church according to his own taste. Was there a Christ? If she knelt before him, what would he say? What would he do? Did Christ have sex? If so, with whom? If not, why not?

The Witch sat in the rear. To her front was the impressive sight of members of the VFW, in white belts and dark blue uniforms. Most were old men, vets from wars gone by. The uniforms were loose in the chest, tight in through the gut. Over the years, men narrowed at the shoulder and broadened at the hip until they began to resemble their women, who,

182

sprouting hairs on their chins, began to resemble their men. Soon they would merge into one being, so that when one of them passed on, the loss would be all the greater. "What's the point, Jesus?" the Witch whispered.

The casket, buried under flowers, was barely visible, and it was closed. The Witch was disappointed. She always enjoyed looking at the dead. The life gone out of it, a body could neither injure nor be injured; it stirred the memory like the sound of rain. Also, since the purpose of a funeral was to bid farewell to the loved one, why close the casket? You didn't shut the door and say good-bye, you said good-bye and shut the door.

She watched Aronson's wife, escorted by her son, wobble down the aisle to the front row. She was a wide-bodied woman, with white hair blued, perhaps to go with her eyes. She didn't look sad as much as frightened, as if she'd wandered into this funeral and discovered, quite by accident, her husband in the coffin. She wore bright red lipstick. The son was long-legged and gangly, a good half a foot taller than his father had been. His face was regular-featured, almost handsome. Behind them walked a blocky young woman, with a faint, embarrassed smile on her face, as if she'd been caught in a lie. This would be the daughter.

The minister said some prayers, and the congregation sang some songs, and then first the son, then the daughter eulogized their father. The son said he hated to see his father die because he was just getting to know him, and now he never would and that was hard to bear. The daughter said the father had gone off to heaven, and she was looking forward to being reunited with him. The son and the daughter avoided eye contact. They hated one another, the Witch could see, and that knowledge made her surge inside with the power of her witchness.

Somewhere along the line, perhaps during some more singing, the Witch lost touch with the ceremony. She was in her memory, remembering that day Aronson had tried to sell her a gun. While she had worked her specialty on him, he had told her a story:

"There was this fellow, name of Ed. Ed developed a nerve problem over his missus leaving him. Run off. Took the kids and everything. Didn't run off with no man. Just *pfttt!* and run off. Which upset Ed, the not knowing why.... Slow down, Witch. I don't want to spout till I finish spouting off. Good, that's better, just right.

"So poor Ed was left alone in his house, which was all right as long as it was daytime or he was drunk. Well, it isn't daytime all day, and a man unless he's a natural-born inebriate won't—can't—stay drunk all the time. During his sober moments, Ed felt uneasy, unreal, un-, like he wasn't all there, like he'd become something you can pass a hand through, a g-d ghost.

"One night Ed happened to look out the window. He noticed a bush his old lady had him plant the year they bought the house. The bush was big and shaggy now. His old lady used to send him out to trim it, and she'd criticize the job he did. You don't make it round, it looks like Woody Woodpecker—stuff like that. Ed got to hate the bush. He was thinking about his hate when, so to speak, he saw his hate staring back at him in the form of a man crouched behind the bush. Ed said to himself, Don't pay no attention—it's all in your head. So he ignored it.

"That night, nothing happened. He had his whiskey, and he forgot the bright eyes in the bush, and he watched the television news, and he went to bed and slept until he had to take a piss at three o'clock in the morning, as per his habit. He took his piss and went back to bed and got up at six-thirty and ate his Wheaties or whatever and drove to work, no bush on his mind.

"Night arrived, as it will, dark, and drunk was Ed, and not particularly unhappy until he looked out the window. The guy behind the bush seared him with those burning eyes. Ed jumped back, spooked out of his jockstrap. When he was composed, he shut off the lights in the house so the guy couldn't see him. ... Thank you, Witch, I was starting to falter, but you got my attention up.

"The eyes in the bush increased in brightness. They were yellow in the bull's-eye, redder toward the outer rings, and black on the edges. You see what he was looking at? Fire. Ed said to himself, This is a Fig Newton of my imagination, and I'm to ignore it. But there was no ignoring those eyes. He drank more whiskey, but no matter how drunk he got, the guy kept staring fire at him from behind the bush.

"Ed went to bed and the crazy idea come to him that the eyes were throwing off some kind rays. Naturally, Ed couldn't sleep, so he prowled about the house in his pajamas. Worked up an anger, and that gave him courage to go outside and face down the guy. Well, as you might guess, there was nobody behind the bush. Next night, same thing. And the next. And so forth.

"This went on for two or three weeks, and Ed was going nuts. He saw a psychiatrist, who asked him about his potty training and gave him some pills. Didn't do no good. Finally, one stormy night the wind was blowing and Ed could hear it racketing against the house. He was especially agitated. By now the man with the burning eyes was permanently camped behind that bush. Ed said, Eeeenough! He went upstairs to the bedroom closet, took out his twelve-gauge pump, loaded her up, opened the front door, and blasted the living hell out of that bush. *Boom! Boom! Boom!*"

At that moment, the Witch's labors drew to an end: Aronson finished. The Witch remembered returning her teeth to her mouth, settling down, rubbing the back of her neck with her hand, and asking, "Then what?"

"What do you mean—then what?"

"You didn't finish the story," the Witch had said.

"Oh, yah, well, I forgot for a sec. I kind of lose interest in these yarns after I get my horn scraped. What happened was he blew the bush to smithereens and killed the man with the burning eyes. There was no body, of course, no blood—but the guy was deader than a fart in a hurricane and his shining eyes were darkened for good. *Boom*—no bush; *boom*—no man; *boom*—no fear. Ed never had any doubt after that. He found himself a nice lady, remarried, and moved to Madison, Wisconsin. You understand the point?"

"That a gun can put soul as well as body to rest," the Witch had said.

Aronson had congratulated himself with a laugh.

Old light from the stars slipped into the room from the window, and the whore's bed was in shadow. The Witch, although she sat in a chair a few feet away, couldn't see the Trans Am, but she guessed he had awakened. His clothes were in a clump on the floor where he had shucked them. Only the knife strapped in leather to his calf remained on his person. She could smell his cologne and something else she couldn't quite identify, an almost imperceptible stink. A change in his breathing, through the mouth instead of the nose, told her for sure he was awake and alert now. She imagined he was thinking about reaching over to touch her; she imagined his hand would pass right through her. She sat perfectly still, silent. She wanted him to think of her as a statue, a monument, a black stone.

"Witch?" he whispered.

She remained motionless.

"Witch!" His shout was shrill, his stink suddenly thick and acrid, so that she knew its source now—anxiety.

She did not move or speak, but tried to connect him to herself by conjuring: *Reach for me, touch me.*

The Trans Am deliberately quieted his breath, signifying he

was a player in her game. Minutes passed. The stink of him became so strong it began to nauseate her. Then she heard the rustling of the sheets and a snap unfasten. What he had reached for was his knife.

"Do you like the dark?" she whispered, just loud enough to be heard.

"You're trying to make me afraid," he said.

"You are afraid," she said.

He moved again, positioning himself to plunge the knife into her. She remained perfectly still, silent. His breathing quickened, and the stink of him was transformed into a strong perfume; he was becoming aroused. She didn't care whether he killed her or not, and she understood it was her indifference that for the moment was saving her life. The thought of the terror in him, his urge to couple and kill, gave form and meaning to her tremor. It doesn't matter about us, she thought. I was lost before I was; he was lost by who he was. More time passed. There was only the sound of their breath, in rhythm now, like two rivers joined. She knew if her silhouette moved a trifle, if her breath caught, if she cried out, he would stab her.

Finally, he moaned. A surrender.

"Someone always dies in your dreams," she said.

"It's never me," he said. At that moment, she flicked on the lamp. Light slashed the room like the brush of some mad painter.

The Trans Am was kneeling on the bed, knife upraised, penis erect. The Witch looked into his eyes. They were like flowers, squeezed into blue droplets.

After they had sex, the Trans Am, calmed, sweet-smelling, lay on his back, the knife resting on his chest, point downward.

"How does it make it you feel?" the Witch asked.

"Important," he said.

"I want to touch the blade," the Witch said.

"Why?"

"For the thrill," she said.

He grasped the handle of the knife but did not remove it from his chest. She put her finger against the blade. His hand moved a trifle, and a blossom of blood appeared on the tip of her index finger.

"Now I'll touch you with my bloody finger," she said.

"I don't know." He was suddenly wary.

"The knife is in your hand, the blood on mine—how can you be afraid?"

"I am not afraid," he said.

She allowed a long moment to pass before she raised her finger and touched him on the forehead.

"Feel it? It doesn't hurt, does it?" she said.

"It's all right—cool." He sat up on the bed and craned his head to see himself in the mirror.

"There's a smear on my forehead," he said.

"The Witch's touch."

They dressed and he sat at her kitchen table drinking ale. After he'd had two bottles, she brought him pictures of Noreen.

"New ones," he said.

"You like them?"

"She's scared," he said.

"Quivers like a bird. Touch her and she'll never stop shaking," the Witch said. She took back the pictures.

"All alone in that bookstore—seems so easy," he said.

"But."

"She's got a boyfriend."

"I know for sure the nights when he won't be around," the Witch said.

14

The Passion of Estelle Jordan

The Witch stole down through the belly of the barn, and slipped the spring lock to the storage room of the porn shop. The darkness inside was like a prison sentence. She groped about until she reached the door to the showroom. She opened it a crack and peeked in. Noreen was prepared to close up for the night. The Witch watched her shut off the outside lights, lock the front door, count the day's receipts, and put the money in a deposit bag. She dragged herself through these chores as one rendered half-conscious by habit and boredom.

Finally, Noreen trudged toward the storage room, to get her things and go home. When the Witch threw open the door, Noreen gave a start.

"Estelle?" Noreen said.

"Not Estelle—the Witch."

"I didn't see you come in. How did you get in? I don't get it." Noreen's voice was charged. This, thought the Witch, is how terror begins: with mystery and wonder.

"Big doings tonight," the Witch said.

Noreen nodded, as if she knew all along what was going to happen to her, although her nod also made it clear she knew nothing and that, in fact, she was pleading for an explanation.

"Turn around," the Witch commanded.

"I don't want to turn around," Noreen said, but she did as she was told.

The Witch ran her fingers along the back of Noreen's neck, then unzipped the red dress with a single pull. Noreen giggled nervously until the Witch pulled the dress over her head. In bra and panties, her body revealed, Noreen was frightened as well as lost.

"I don't like this—I don't like the strangeness." Noreen's voice quivered.

"You're scared—I can feel it," the Witch said.

"I don't get it," Noreen said.

"Just think about how you feel at this moment," the Witch said.

"I'm afraid—you've made me afraid."

"A minute ago, out there, you were dead. Now you're alive, every nerve tingling."

"I trusted you, now you're hurting me."

"Trust comes easy-like, trust begs a mother for her love," the Witch said. "A trap. Survive trust and you might live a long time."

The Witch brushed Noreen's cheek with her lips. Noreen's fear tripped through the Witch like some powerful drug taking hold; the Witch grew strong and terrible.

"Lie down," the Witch said.

Noreen lay supine on the floor.

"On her back—it figures," the Witch said. "Turn over."

The Witch bound Noreen's wrists and ankles, using the plastic twine that bundled the dirty magazines. Noreen struggled, but like a lamb in the jaws of a wolf: her terror had denied her the full use of her muscles.

Her work finished for the moment, the Witch strutted about. Then, half dancing, she stripped naked, leaving her skirt, blouse, and work lace on the floor beside Noreen, who had begun to weep softly.

190

"Not bad, eh? You like?" The Witch addressed an imaginary audience, as she thrust out her loins.

She picked up Noreen's red dress, dangling it before Noreen's face, before wiggling into it. Noreen stopped weeping. The Witch said tauntingly, "The wasp puts on the butterfly's wings."

"My dress! That's my dress." Outrage drained some of the fear from Noreen and gave her courage.

"You don't own nothing, Noreen." The witch pranced about the room, posing in the dress, mocking the gestures of a fashion model.

"What are you going to do with me?" The fear in Noreen returned, redoubled. She spoke not to, but beyond, the Witch, as one praying.

"For the time being, shut you up." The Witch ghosted into the showroom. Behind the counter she found a gag consisting of black leather ribbons and a red rubber ball. With this she muffled Noreen. Trussed and silenced, Noreen lay unmoving on the storage-room floor.

Shutting the storage-room door behind her, alone now in the main part of the store, the Witch began to test herself in the red dress, standing stock-still, trying to feel contact with this body that, as it seemed, was not hers and that was draped by this dress that was not hers either. An image passed through her mind of a girl waiting on the streetcorner for boys to drive by.

The porn shop looked different, as if she'd never been here before. It disgusted her. There seemed to be a permanent smell of piss in the air. Walls were smudged, floors grimy, magazine racks weighed down, the reading matter limp from handling.

In spite of herself, as if guided by an inner command she had no control over, she gathered up a sack of tokens to play the peep shows. The cramped, ramshackle booths evoked a memory of bob houses for ice fishing. Every fall Isaac built a new one, each less well constructed than the previous year's model. He might have saved himself the trouble by taking in the current year's structure before the ice broke up in March or April, but he never got around to it. Sometimes Estelle visited, enjoying the brightness of the frozen pond. Isaac chopped holes in the ice, baited his lines with minnows, rigged the tip-ups, and retired to the comfort of the bob house. He'd sit on a wooden bench, warmed by a fire in a five-gallon milk jug he'd converted into a wood heater. His pleasure was to sip whiskey and watch the weather through a tiny window. "Don't know why but the booze tastes better out here," he'd say, gesturing with the bottle.

She moved from one hard bench to another in the movie booths, dropping in tokens, letting the movies unreel in concert. The booths and the films, like the rest of the porn shop, were worn and shabby. Scribblings marred the walls. Holes had been gouged through to the neighboring booths. Film projectors groaned from overuse and poor maintenance. There were breakdowns in the showings. (The projector ground on while the picture vanished, or the image was gauzy, or there was no projector noise, no picture, nothing but a lost token.) The films themselves were fuzzy, nicked, scarred. It seemed to the Witch that even the performers had aged, as a result not of the passage of time but of the weather in this place. Back-of-the Barn Adult Books 'n' Flicks was growing old, dying.

She searched for that girl who had gypped the men, paid with her body and, perhaps, her life. She never found her.

She left the peep shows and, rummaged about the porn shop, tearing off the plastic covers and looking at dirty magazines. Dazed as if by the sun, she unexpectedly found herself staring into one of the mirrors planted to scare off customers from shoplifting. The mirror was curved, distorting her image.

"Noreen?" A hand in the mirror reached toward her own hand, and she jerked it away. Once again she felt Noreen's

192

fear flow into her, except instead of filling her with strength as it had before, it now drained the strength from her like a fast-overtaking illness. In a moment, she was panicky and frightened, feeling precisely the emotions she herself had foisted upon Noreen earlier. Fear made everything difficult. It was difficult to think, difficult to act. She had to breathe deliberately and deeply to keep from fleeing. Yet she managed to prepare for the Trans Am. She unlocked the door to the customer entry, leaving it half open, and took her place on the stool behind the counter.

Perhaps ten minutes had gone by when she heard the throaty purr of the car pulling into the parking lot.

She remained on the stool, legs crossed, hands together. She didn't have to look to know when he'd entered the store. She could smell the anxiety on him. She turned and faced him. He stood, masked, knife in hand.

"Witch—where's the other one? You promised me the other one." He was shocked to see her.

"I am the other one." Her voice was soaked with fear. Her Witch's tremor flowed to the Trans Am.

The dress had been worn and washed so much, the fibers that held it together were weakened, so when the Trans Am grasped the front of it, it parted down the middle as if by magic, soundlessly and all at once. Naked, the Witch huddled in a small S on the floor. From the beginning, she understood this was not to be one of those teach-you-a-lesson beatings. Such beatings were delivered by hand, like embraces gone mad. The Trans Am's means would be his boots; he aimed to mutilate and destroy her. It was that certainty, the sudden calm it brought her as she succumbed to it, that made her realize human hope was the most ruinous of lies. She felt free, on the verge of something new.

With the first blow, her fear vanished. She felt a thudding

193

against her flesh, but no pain as such. Sounds—his grunts, her moans—seemed to come from loudspeakers. The porn shop, the Trans Am in his mask, were bright and clear, if jarring. It was as if someone were shaking the sun. She found herself almost entertained by the heavy swinging boots, as if she were watching a movie screen and the blows reached through the screen to her own face and body. She felt no compulsion to protect herself. She wished only to remain conscious to appreciate what was happening. She understood the beating itself as a message, not directed toward her in particular but toward all living creatures. The beating said: A life is given meaning by its end. So be it. To save herself, she had both to destroy herself and to save Noreen. This, her sacrifice of the body of the old whore, was her means.

Time passed, she didn't know how much. She glimpsed her teeth on the floor, smashed.

After a while, the Trans Am grew tired. The thudding stopped; he gasped for breath. She watched him reach for his face, as if to attack it. Next, she heard the *rip* sound of parting Velcro, and the mask peeled from his skull like a second flesh. Beneath, his soft-hard, smooth face was soaked with sweat. As if blinded, he reached around him, and came up with the dress. He wiped his face on it.

He crouched over her, peering at her. She lay unmoving. He pinched the nipple of one of her breasts, and when she did not respond, he unfastened the belt to his pants. She understood now that he would rape her, but that he had wanted to wait until her body was limp, lifeless, completely under his command. He pawed at her, his touch glacial, impersonal as if he were fondling one of the inflatable dolls on sale at the porn shop.

His prick entering her was cold and hard. There was no passion in him, no desire—only will. The porn shop grew

194

THE PASSION OF ESTELLE JORDAN

quiet. She thought for a moment she was in a church, attending a funeral, her wandering mind conjuring this place, this end, with this maniac. *Where am I? Help me, Mother.* And she was sitting on a stool and a woman (was it her mother?) was making up her face, talking to her, telling her the secrets of her life.

A long time ago, Noreen, I had a social disease. Doctor examined me, says, "You're scarred inside." I says, "I'll say." He says, "You can't have any more children." My body told me otherwise. I had another. Willow. Only he wasn't made for this world. Hollered for his soul, for the Jordan soul. Willow, my youngest, was sired by Ollie, my oldest, when he was fifteen. Willow was Ollie's and Willow was mine. Oliver used to beat Willow because he was made wrong and because Oliver had a good idea where he came from. Ollie would protect Willow. At the time, I didn't care about Willow or about anything. I was in never-never land, like you're in now, Noreen—like they hit you and it doesn't hurt.

One day there was a fight. I watched it. I watched my eldest son murder his father to save my youngest son. Ollie, after he done the deed to Oliver, he got wisdom. He saw the truth. Which soon, in the glaring pain of it, he was to forget. But at that moment, when he understood, he named me. "Witch— you're the Witch," he says. When I had the name, I assumed the self. When Ollie and I made Willow, pity for myself told me we had fallen in together as kin will, victims of happenstance. How pity lies. Witchness made me see the truth. I used Ollie to rid myself of Oliver. Witchness bore me an eye for seeing the world as it is. I've paid the price for knowledge. Donald denies me. No Witch gave him birth; the Witch is barren. It was that girl back then that gave birth to four sons. You, Noreen.

My life is over, my story made. Never mind that the facts

195

will be changed in the telling; I will give the kinship new heart.
After the flesh of me is gone I'll live in the stories, rekindling
the kinship, destroyed by it, creating it.

The Witch came to consciousness in degrees. She was on
the homestead farm Isaac had failed at, listening to pigs grunt.
The sounds reminded her of sex, and she was fifteen with a
customer. And finally she was pushing sixty, here, in the porn
shop, listening to the Trans Am reaching his climax. The tremor
dies forever at this moment, she thought. As the Trans Am
finished, the Witch's body shifted involuntarily and his face
came into full contact with her own. His lips on her sunken
mouth tasted like slushy snow from the street.

She felt him jerk away in revulsion and leap to his feet. As
he buttoned his pants he saw her blood on his hands. He
reached for his face, feeling it. More blood. He picked up the
dress and again wiped his face, tossing the dress casually away.
It fell beside Estelle. Slowly, the image on the dress came into
focus. The Witch's face was imprinted on the dress. The dear
self reached out.

The movement took the Trans Am by surprise. He knocked
her hand away. With a grunt, he returned the mask to his
face, and stepped back. He circled her suspiciously, like a
starving animal appraising poison meat. She never saw him
go for the knife strapped to his leg; it blossomed from his hand,
a silver flower. He knelt beside her, keeping a distance. Curious, frightened, he stared at her for the longest time. He
crept a little closer and began poking the knife at her belly.
She could feel the belly respond, like a wave. His eyes widened
in horror.

"Something in there," he said, and screamed, his familiar
lost-boy scream.

Just before she blacked out again, she saw him raise the
knife to plunge it into her belly.

* * *

Critter awaited Delphina's homemade pizza, prepared according to the Jordan formula—store-bought crust, store-bought tomato sauce, salt, pepper, oregano, garlic powder, upon which was piled grated cheddar cheese and the key ingredient, ground venison. Critter traded for game meat with Abenaki, who was a wild and peculiar man, even by Jordan standards. The only time of year Abenaki didn't hunt was during the legal deer-killing season in November, when, as he would say, "It ain't safe to be in the woods." Critter himself was no hunter, but could honestly say he liked hunting. He found neither profit nor comfort in tramping about in dark, gloomy forests, and he didn't like getting up early in the morning only to go out in the cold, and, although he wouldn't admit it even to himself, killing animals made him squeamish. What Critter liked most about hunting were the tools of the hunter—guns and knives. Not that he desired to shoot or cut anything. It was just that weapons pleased his eye, as painted pictures might have pleased the eye of another man.

"Smells ready," he prodded.

"Another couple of minutes," Delphina said.

He stiffened, as one suffering an inadvertent insult. It was a gesture that never failed to infuriate his wife.

"Another...couple...of minutes." Delphina was trying to avoid a fight.

"You always say that and you always burn the cheese." Critter delivered this criticism impartially as a judge.

"Serve it up yourself, then." Delphina stormed out of the kitchen.

The tone in her voice (which said, "Shut up, grouch!") revealed to Critter his hidden mood beneath the lighthearted glaze of drink—anger.

Slapped numb by five beers, Critter should have been happy. Why am I so on edge? he silently asked the empty beer bottle in front of him. No answer came, but he was left with

197

a vague resentment against Delphina for making him draw attention to his depths. Noreen wouldn't have done that. Noreen adored him.

Something formed in his mind, a question. Why did distance between man and wife increase as they drew closer? Because of the beer, or perhaps because of himself (Critter wouldn't have been able to say which), the question never quite formed entirely in his mind. It settled in unconstituted to tease him, like a familiar name forgotten but on the tip of the tongue. He suffered the itch of uncertainty.

"Del?" he called.

"What do you want now?" she shouted from the living room. She'd turned on the television.

"Nothing," he said.

He knew one thing that was bothering him, the affair with Noreen. It wasn't so much that she was making demands — the CB, the VCR. He didn't much like spending his hard-earned cash for someone else's pleasure, but he'd foot the bill as he would any other for services rendered. In one sense, he welcomed her demands; they demonstrated to him that he had means, she value. What bothered him was the habit of two women; it was overtaking him, like drink or smoke. He didn't need one more bad habit. (He'd started thinking of his life in terms of habits because the word *habit* didn't have any tender hooks in it.) Not that he wanted to break the habit. He wanted to continue: Delphina at his side, Noreen on the side. The fact was, he'd been relatively content of recent. But like any contented man conscious of his contentment, it was the consciousness of the contentment that, ultimately, discontented him.

If only he didn't have this urge to tell Delphina everything. He was always on the verge of confessing, even while he knew how stupid and fruitless a confession would be. The trouble was his own vanity. He wanted both to tuck it to Delphina, so to speak, by showing her he couldn't be taken for granted, and to unburden himself emotionally. He might be happy, but lately he was also pent up. He needed relief—confession would bring it. But if he confessed, he'd lose not only one of his women, or perhaps both, but his secret. He'd be empty again, the way he was before he took up with Noreen. More than Delphina's wrath, more than the real possibility that she would leave him and separate him from the family that meant so much to him, more than the loss of Noreen, more than the loss of love itself, what Critter feared most was emptiness.

"Del?—Del!"

"What?"

"Serve it up, goddamn it!"

She didn't exactly come running, but she did come, and the pizza was not burnt, and after a few bites he felt a little more at peace.

"Can I get you a beer?" he asked.

Delphina, dear wife, recognized his attempt to smooth relations. "I could use a beer," Delphina answered civilly, and sat at the table.

After a time, she said, "You're so uptight. Honestly, but I think you work too hard. You're never home."

"Miss me?"

"Well, yes—well, not always. Things seem to go better when you're not around. It's like I've got one less child to deal with."

He might have hit her then, reached out without a thought and batted her one right side of the head, but the phone rang. It was Dot McCurtin, Darby's high-tech town gossip.

"There's an emergency call for you on the CB, sounds like the real thing," Mrs. McCurtin said.

Moments later Critter was listening to Noreen's voice, "Red Dress calling Van Man, Red Dress calling Van Man. Emergency! Emergency!"

Seconds after Noreen explained the situation—some sex

199

maniac working over the Witch in the bookstore—Critter was in the van with Crowbar, speeding toward the auction barn.

"Red Dress, this is Van Man. On the road, to the rescue. Over."

"I think he's killed her." Noreen's voice quivered through the static of the CB.

"Red Dress, name your present location? Over."

"Why, Critter—I'm in my car in the parking lot." Even through her fear, Noreen's tone carried just a suggestion of Delphina's brand of sarcasm, and Critter twitched inside with annoyance.

"Red Dress, get out of there. Start your engine and drive away. Over."

"I can't, I'm too scared. Over."

"If he comes out of the bookstore, he'll see you, and you'll be dead meat. Red Dress, can you run? Over."

"I can run."

"Get out of car, Red Dress, and go hide. Run in the woods. Find a dark place, lay down and wait for the sound of my voice. And, Red Dress, don't move once you lie down. Don't make noises. Over. Red Dress? Red Dress? Over. Noreeeeeen?"

Noreen did not respond.

He'd told her to get out. Had she fled the car? If so, why hadn't she signed off? Critter was really concerned now. He reached in the glove compartment of the van, knowing there was nothing there that could help him, but all the same—reaching. His father used to carry a .357 magnum pistol in the glove compartment, and Critter couldn't get the notion out of his head that somehow the gun would materialize for his reaching hand. When his hand found only paper, Critter felt betrayed.

By now the CB airways were crackling with the peculiar accent of Jordans, a Yankee twang slowed down by a drawl almost Southern in its leisure. The Witch was in trouble. Any Jordan man in the Darby area who had a car or truck in running condition was headed for the barn on Route 21. Even Donald and his junkyard crew, twelve miles away in Tuckerman, had got the message and started their engines.

Critter knew he'd be the first to arrive at the barn. He had no gun; the smart thing to do would be to wait for help only minutes behind. Yet he did not. Something in him was changing second by second. Concern gave way to worry, worry to panic, panic to fear, fear to anger, anger to rage, rage to desire, desire to ecstasy, until he felt everything he'd ever felt in his life all at once; he was bathed in a pure emotional light—and then one thing, one emotion, something he'd never felt before, a single-minded will to do, soul to dare. His vision and mental processes narrowed, concentrated. He could see better, think more clearly; for the moment, the clutter of his life was broomed away in a shower of sparks.

He thought: Get the sex maniac, kill him. Nothing else mattered. He was no longer the husband and father, the businessman and employer, the American bent on happiness and prosperity—cautious, logical, worrisome, cunning. He was a pure Jordan male loosed on the world—headstrong, unpredictable, fearless, direct, dangerous, deadly.

In the seconds after he'd pulled off the blacktop into the auction-barn drive, he formed a plan, a Jordan plan. He had no weapon—no gun, no knife; nothing but Crowbar. And this van. By Jawj, this van could do a number on a guy. He had the van and the dog—and surprise. With no thought given to the consequences, he wheeled into the parking lot, aimed the van at the customer entry of Back-of-the-Barn Adult Books 'n' Flicks, and crashed through the wall.

The van plowed in a good six feet, taking down the door, ripping through frame lumber, plywood, sheetrock, and siding.

A split second later Critter and Crowbar jumped out of the cab into a cloud of dust. Critter saw a guy in a mask, dazed for a moment, and he saw a knife on the floor.

"Get him!" shouted Critter, and Crowbar attacked. The guy ran outside, Crowbar after him barking and snarling.

On the floor lay the Witch, bleeding, naked, oddly vibrating. And then it was as if the Witch had risen up from that battered body, and stood young, beautiful, and cruel. Critter raised his hands to his face, resisting the urge to cover his eyes. A picture flashed in his mind of his son Ollie playing peek-a-boo. He saw now that it was Noreen standing before him. She was wearing the Witch's clothes.

"She saved me, and I saved her." Noreen measured out her words as she spoke them. Critter wondered whether she was stoned. He couldn't get it out of his mind that the Noreen he knew was gone, vaporized, that this person was not Noreen but the Witch in a new form.

A movement from the Witch caught his attention. He watched her belly ripple. Critter had never seen muscles behave that way. Alarmed, he stepped back. The Witch began to pant furiously, her belly as alive as a lake in a storm, and then the waves subsided and soon she was breathing almost normally. He continued to watch, fascinated, stupefied, as the ripples on the belly began to build up again.

"What is this?" he said, more to himself than to Noreen.

"Birth—she's borning something." Noreen's face glistened.

Critter couldn't remember picking up the knife. It merely appeared in his hand. He held it like the Statue of Liberty her torch. The next thing he knew he was running outside through the hole in the wreckage. Moonlight lit up the parking lot. The masked guy backpedaled toward his car, Crowbar menacing him. Critter strode forward, knife held high.

The guy in the mask made it to his car, but too late. Abenaki

202

Jordan piled into the parking lot with his pickup truck and blocked his exit. Critter and Abenaki pulled the guy out of the car. Critter had expected a fight, but the guy's limbs were like water. He was scared shitless.

Other Jordans arrived, and soon a dozen men stood around, penning in the guy in the mask, pushing him around.

Without consciously meaning to, the group moved as one back toward the bookstore. Bright, blue-white light poured through the hole in the wreckage. As one spying, Critter watched his Uncle Donald kneel on the floor beside the Witch. He saw the Witch's hand reach up and Donald enclose it within his own hands.

For Critter, everything brightened, time accelerated. The night, the situation, seemed unreal; the idea of material being had lost credibility. It was a feeling he welcomed. He felt in control, as one feels in control of a dream, even as it sweeps one out to its sea. He spotted Abenaki, Andre, and Alsace, and he grabbed his half-brothers by the scruffs of their necks. "Let's get him!" he shouted, dragging his brothers with him, as he bulled his way forward and grabbed the mask. The sound of it torn from the face rippled pleasingly through Critter's fingertips.

It was the Acheson kid. Upper Darby snot. Critter hit him in the face, swinging with his forearm so the butt end of the knife handle caught the kid flush. Blood blossomed from his mouth. The kid made no sound; his eyes rolled. He was like a deer brought down by dogs, beyond apprehension, beyond fear, awaiting his end. Critter didn't want to look at the face. He stepped back. "Andre, put the mask back on his face," Critter ordered. Andre hesitated, and Alsace stepped in and did the job. Blood dripped through the mouth zipper.

Donald emerged from the wreckage, carrying the Witch blanketed in his arms. Donald, the Witch, Noreen, and Donald's son, Again, drove off. Critter felt a strange, unaccountable anger, as if something had been taken from him and he didn't even know what it was.

Somebody mentioned telephoning Constable Perkins, but Critter shouted, "No, he's mine."

"Abenaki, you and Alsace put that guy in the back seat," Critter commanded. "I'll drive his car. Andre, you follow us in my van. Everybody else go home."

Critter wasn't sure what he was going to do next, but he knew he didn't want the kid and the car on his own property.

He liked the feel of the Trans Am, not sure and steady like his van or dignified and powerful like his Caddy, but hard and responsive—violent. He drove fast, like a drunk teenager enjoying the feeling of speed. Impulsively, he turned off on Upper Darby Road, roared right past the Acheson place and finally into the Salmon Trust lands.

The road was dirt now, and Critter began to feel himself surge from the inside. He cut the wheel of the Trans Am, and the car barreled into the woods. Abenaki hollered with glee as the car bounced and jounced, plowing through small trees. Critter hollered, imitating Abenaki—*eeeeyow!* Crowbar joined in. Then all the Jordans, maddened and ecstatic, hollered at once.

The Trans Am only went about fifty feet before it got stuck, a big rock under the oil pan, the front end sticking up so the headlights shined into the sky.

"Now what?" said Abenaki from the back seat of the Trans Am. His breath came in lusty gasps. Andre ran from Critter's van, shouting, "Gimme a go at him!" And Alsace answered, "I'll have a turn, I'll have a turn."

Critter spoke the words, "Pull down his pants," and showed the knife before he himself understood his own intentions.

"This is not your lucky day," Abenaki said, and pawed at the Acheson lad, like some deranged lover.

204

The Acheson kid began to struggle now, whimper and wriggle and whine. Crowbar, as if in mockery, mimicked the whine.

Critter surged with power and strength. He climbed into the back seat, and by himself turned the Acheson kid upside down. Once they got the kid's pants over his hips, it took only a couple of seconds to complete the job. Critter grabbed the kid's balls and with one slice of the knife set them free, letting them drop to the floor of the car. The kid wasn't even sure what had happened.

They laughed as he ran screaming into the dark woods.

Critter fetched the siphon hose from the van. They drew out a couple of gallons of gas from the Trans Am, doused the inside, and touched it off. Whitish headlamp glow seemed to jet off into the night from the orange flames.

After leaving his kinsman at the barn where their respective vehicles were parked, Critter drove himself and Crowbar home. He didn't know whether the Witch was dead or alive; didn't care really. It didn't matter. As for himself and Noreen, their affair was over. That didn't matter either. What mattered was the future of the kinship—himself, Delphina, Little Ollie, Jawj, and other children he would sire.

When he arrived home, he was still full of energy, alert and powerful. He stormed into the house, walking right past Delphina into the bathroom. He rummaged through the medicine cabinet until he found her birth-control pills. He flung the plastic tin on the floor and stomped it with his heel.

15

Peace

Because her eyes were closed, Estelle Jordan felt more than saw the gold light of morning. *Touch the light.* She reached. Her hand moved from the blanket into the bar of sunlight. The shadow of her hand falling across her face, obscuring the daylight through her closed eyelids, caused her to cross from sleep to wakefulness, and she opened her eyes. A few words from the voice in the dream remained—*Touch the light.* She experienced a moment of mild regret at having lost something.

She arose, opened the window of her bedroom, breathed in the morning air, looked far at the greening hills, listened far for crows, looked near at the huge maple tree—she thrilled to the fright of its new foliage—listened near to chickadees. These birds of May, squabbling, complaining, happy in their violence—what optimists they were. They made her feel optimistic herself. Time of year, she thought. Everything new. She watched the birds, listened to them, felt them in her heart. They were a pattern to appreciate, like the faded design of an old quilt, or the lines in a pair of hands, or the rhythm of an old man snoring. And that made her think of Avalon Hillary. He'd telephoned her, asked to drop by late in the morning for coffee.

She dressed in loose-fitting blue jeans, a plain cotton blouse, ankle-top work shoes (the kind that poor girl she'd left behind

206

had stitched years ago in the shoe shop); she brushed her hair, tying it into a ponytail; she washed her face but applied no makeup to it.

Avalon arrived at ten A.M., a bunch of dried weeds in his fist. "Last year's growth," he said.

"Thought you were partial to the green stuff," she kidded.

"I am," Avalon said.

"But you knew I liked them dry and brown." She arranged the weeds in a wooden pot. "You look good, Avalon, trim, cleaned up, new clothes."

"You look good, too, Estelle." He choked on the words, and his eyes said, "My, how she has aged."

She understood. She had seen the figure in the mirror. Almost overnight, her hair had turned nearly white. Deep furrows cut into her face. Her hips had widened and her shoulders were rounding.

"You still can't tell a lie with any conviction," Estelle said.

Avalon blushed. "You had a hard winter, I know, but I guess you're going to make it for a few more years."

"I intend to. I've got one more life to live."

And as before when they were lovers and friends, they chatted for a few minutes. Which was to say that Avalon talked. Things were going well. He'd found a way to get out from under the farm and still keep his land. He'd gone into partnership with a Mr. Charles Barnum, a Tuckerman lawyer; they planned to open a nine-hole golf course.

"I need to keep busy, and this should do it. I said to the landscape architect, 'You decide how to remodel the terrain as you please, but I kind of like that stuck-in-the-mud backhoe where it is. Gives me humility.' He says, 'We can incorporate it in the course as a hazard.' I says, 'A hazard—well, yes.'" Avalon chuckled, enjoying his joke immensely.

Finally, Avalon got around to the personal stuff. "I'm seeing the widow Kringle. We're talking about making it permanent, being we're both used to matrimony. I didn't want you to hear it from somebody else. You did a lot for this old gander, kept him upstanding when he was about to keel over."

"It's better you go with her, better for you, better for me. I'm getting out of the man business—no more customers, no more boyfriends."

"You'll have to make ends meet," Avalon said. "I'll give you a job in the clubhouse."

She knew he'd honor that promise, and hate like Hades seeing her day after day. "The Witch was no fool," she said. "The Witch put away a few dollars. And anyway, I'm a Jordan—taken care of. What with a new baby on the way, Critter's starting a new business, a handy mart in place of the bookstore. I'll be clerking part-time—nights. I always did like night work."

"I don't quite know how to put it in words, Estelle, but I knew what was said about you—I knew what you were. But when I looked at you, I saw another walking beside you."

He didn't embrace her as he left, but backed out of the front door with the mixture of magnificence and awkwardness of one of his bovines backing out of a stall.

The outside dinned. The birds had gone to war. She saw beauty in even their noise and violence. Was there any creature that didn't inflict pain on its own kind? "No—no, siree," she answered herself. The beauty she beheld—was it out there? "No—no, siree. In here." She thumped her chest.

Beauty was the great discovery of her recuperation. Privacy had become solitude, escape had become awareness, of growing things, design, color: beauty. Beauty: which through the very fact that it was not substance and therefore could not be worn out made her aware of herself as flesh, bone, blood, of the sadness of the frailty and impermanence of the human body. Beauty: which was both surrender and conquest. Beauty hurt and healed at the same time. You pricked your finger and it hurt, and a little bubble of blood blossomed into a rose and the fragrance sustained you as well as any food.

She slow-danced through her apartment to feel the beauty of the dear self moving. She fiddled with her plants, to take in their beauty. She fingered through a book until she found a fern, pressed between the pages. She crumbled it in her fingers to feel the dryness, to feel the loss of it in her heart as it turned to dust. She enjoyed a sense of righteousness, of God-almighty light. She spoke, but inwardly. "This that I have, my experience, this dust, teaches me, makes me. Destruction of something beautiful, if it be done with appreciation of the beauty, preserves the thing."

She was geting ready to go out, drive to Donald's house, when the phone rang. It was one of her customers.

"Heard you were in the hospital, laid up for most of the winter," he said, his voice jovial as any salesman's.

"That's so," Estelle said.

"You're home now, though."

"That's so—I'm home."

"You, ah, have a free night soon?"

"My nights were never free. Now they're all free."

"Oh, are they now?" The make-believe cheer vanished from his voice.

Estelle headed him off before he got too mad. "Hang on," she said, genuine cheer in her own voice. "You're not wasting your time. Fact is, this old girl is retired, but I can recommend a lady who can help you out. Trained her myself. She costs a little more. But, listen—young stuff. Think about it."

After she'd finished talking to the customer, she called No-reen.

"I'm sending you another one," she said. "Here's the story on him..."

When Estelle left for Tuckerman, the sun was high in the

sky, showering the leaves with bright, silvery sparks. She paused for a moment on the landing, almost expecting to see the Trans Am. A car could be resurrected from his ashes via insurance. As for the young driver, who could tell? If medical science could find a way to sew the quick back onto a fellow, he'd be out there again terrible as ever. A shiver of fear ran through her. She did not deny it. She would know the world, all of it, good and evil joined, as she, the Witch and the dear self, were joined. So be it. This feeling, this knowledge, this memory shadow of the tremor, was not entirely unpleasant.

When she arrived at Donald's house, instead of taking her place at the head of the table in the kitchen, she walked down to the garage. She ignored Donald's rule banning women in the shop and entered it. Donald stood beside a shiny black car, the welding torch in his hand, mask down. Sparks flew; the light was white and blinding. She shut her eyes. When she opened them it was as if a great span of time had passed; she *was* new. The light from Donald's torch went out. He turned toward her and lifted the mask to his forehead, and she could see his face. In his eyes she recognized a tenderness for her.

So, she thought, this is my peace.